My Tales Growing Up In Long Beach

Stories For My Daughters

A Baby Boomer's Tale

Second Printing

Chuck Mosley

ISBN-978-1-79907-008-5

DEDICATION

This Book is dedicated to Melissa, Mandi and Cari

For their love and support

Contents

ACKNOWLEDGMENTS

I'd like to acknowledge my Facebook page and Growing Up In Long Beach friends for their comments and encouragement to put my stories into a book. I'd also like to thank Vince Prugh for his help with formatting and editing and Jimmy Scott for his encouragement to keep moving forward.

Forward

My Tales Growing Up In Long Beach

This book is a series of stories about my memories of growing up. They were written over a two-year period and were individual stories written on their own. Although I tried to place them in a sequential order, there is overlapping of time and events in certain stories. So please enjoy each chapter as an individual event in our childhoods.

Chapter 1 -- April 26, 1951

I was born at 3:20 am, April 26, 1951, at Bixby Knolls Hospital. Mom was 17 and my father was 18. My parents met while attending Lindberg Junior High School and continued dating at Jordan High School in north Long Beach. They both dropped out of Jordan in their senior year when my Mom became pregnant with me.

My Dad already had a trade, a body and fender man. He had been working for his dad and had learned his trade early. During his high school years he was always buying cars, fixing or customizing them and then selling for a profit! When I came along, my Dad had customized a 2-door, '40 Ford sedan with chopped top, chrome reverse wheels with baby moon hubcaps, twin chrome spotlights, fender skirts, shaved door handles and a dark blue paint job!

My Mom once borrowed my Dad's car and the battery died. She could not get out of the car until someone noticed she was stranded...with the chopped top and electric solenoids to open the doors she was stuck! As my birth approached my Dad had to sell the '40! He bought a vacant lot in north Long Beach on Harding St., just east of Cherry, and they built a duplex at the age of 18 yrs. old!

When I was 4, my folks sold the duplex and bought a new house in Rolling Hills in Palos Verdes. I started my education at Hillside Elementary School. It was also brand new. I had a friend, Scotty, whom I would meet at his house and walk to school together. His house was on the way and we could go out his back gate and follow a dirt trail down the hill to school.

One morning, after a night of rain, I was dressed in a pair of new white pants and a tan shirt for school. My Mom told me to be sure and stay on the sidewalk all the way to school. Well, naturally, when I met Scotty, we went out his back gate to the dirt trail. I took about a dozen steps and then slid all the way down the hill in the mud! My white pants now covered in mud! I proceeded back to my house, crying at the door so as not to get into too much trouble!

I also met my first girlfriend in kindergarten, a really cute girl, Cathy! Unfortunately, she made me a cake on our third date 12 years later...

On Saturday mornings my brother, Chris, and I would saddle-up and ride along with the cowboys on TV, the early westerns starring John Wayne and Gabby Hayes, Gene Autry and Champion and Roy and Trigger! We would gallop along, using the armrests of the sofa as our horses and Dad's belts as our reins and ropes! As the action increased so did the action in the living room! Being shot out of the saddle and landing on the cushions strategically placed on the floor was fun and happened routinely! I could also jump across the couch and pull my brother off his horse and we'd "fight" each other just like on TV!

In 1956 when I'd come home from kindergarten, I would watch the Mickey Mouse Club. Of course my favorite was Spin and Marty and their adventures on the Triple R Ranch! I was in love with their horse Skyrocket!

My parents decided that they'd like to try the country life. My grandfather had sold his garage, "Hollydale Motors," and bought 40 acres in Elsinore, growing hay and wheat, and raising cows, goats and of course, he had a horse! My folks purchased 2 1/2 acres from my grandfather and built a new house.

My Dad was working at McKenzie Ford in Long Beach (10th & Long Beach Blvd.) in the body shop and planned on finding work in Elsinore. I was really excited to move to the country and get my own pony! All I could think of was a bridle with silver chains between the bit and the reins, just like Roy had for Trigger! When the house was finished, we moved in, and I started school, first grade, in a one-room schoolhouse, kindergarten through sixth grade. The school building was old, something you'd see on "Little House on the Prairie."

I had a couple cousins I had never met in my classroom and two aunts in the junior high next door! My parents bought me the pony and the bridle I wanted, just like on TV! And. of course, I named him Skyrocket.

I wanted to ride him to school so bad, but was told I was just too young! My Dad never got a job in Elsinore and spent the next year driving back and forth to Long Beach, a very long commute without freeways! So when my first grade was finished, the decision to move back to Long Beach was made. I remember looking at a couple smaller houses in the Virginia Country Club area, but they chose a house on Pasadena and 46th Streets in Bixby Knolls, the house in which I spent the rest of my childhood.

We moved in a week or two before I was to start 2nd grade at Los Cerritos Elementary School. The morning after we were settled, there was a knock on the door. I opened the door and there stood two kids about my age! Hi, I'm Rich, and this is my brother, Bob. We live up the street! How old are you? Where are you from? What grade are you? Are you going to Los Cerritos? Do you know how to play baseball???

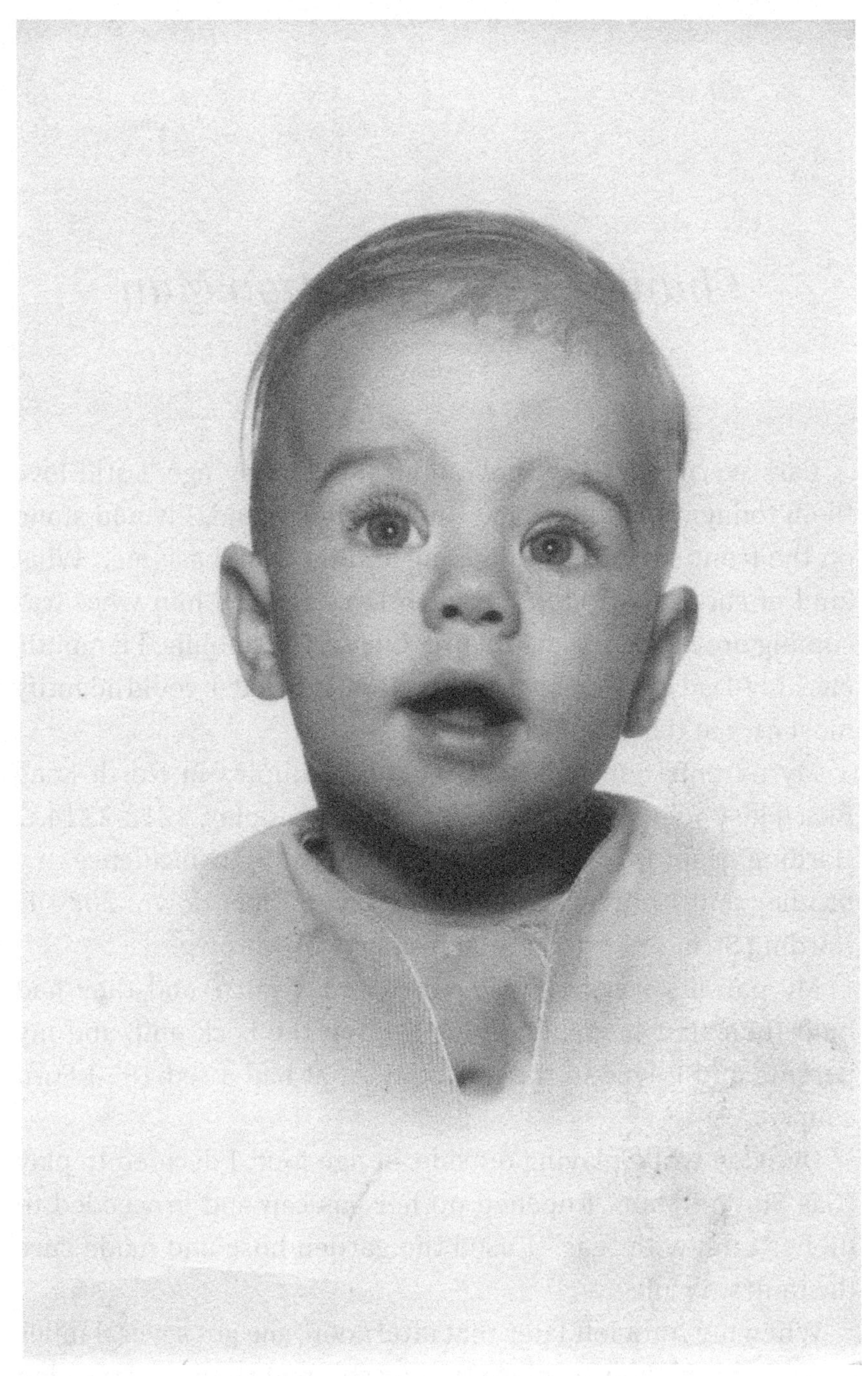

Chapter 2 -- Gas Station Man

Cars were what I was all about at an early age. I still love them today. When I was four and five years old, I would stand on the front seat next to my Dad, and he would ask me, "What kind of car is that?" I would then look and tell him what was coming down the street, "a Ford, Chevy, Oldsmobile, Plymouth, etc." My Dad took great pride in the fact that I could identify most cars at that age.

My parents bought a lot and built a duplex in North Long Beach just before I was born in 1951. The duplex, 2212-2214 E. Harding, right off of Cherry, is still there. By coincidence, my brother and I purchased a duplex several lots down, 2030 E. Harding St. in 1979 as a rental property of our own.

My parents were only 17 when I was born, and they had built their first home. My Aunt lived in the back unit, and my parents and I lived in the front. My Aunt had a red 1950 Ford coupe.

One day while playing outside, at age four, I decided to play "Gas Station Man." I opened up her gas cap and proceeded to fill her tank with "gas." I used the garden hose and made sure the tank was full.

When my Aunt left later that afternoon, she got several miles away from the house before the car stopped running. Stranded and unable to get the car to start, she called my Dad for assistance. They soon determined that I had filled it up with "gas" from the garden hose.

A few months later my Dad was working in the garage and he placed me in the car so I could pretend I was driving. Well, the car had a three-speed transmission, and the starter was a button on the floor next to the gas pedal.

Dad had left the car parked in first gear, as was common practice, and I made my way to the floor and pressed on the starter. Each time I pressed on the starter the car lurched forward. I kept pressing the starter until the car lurched and crashed through the single car garage door. My father was rather embarrassed, as he was working in the garage helping a neighbor, who happened to be a Long Beach Policeman. It seems like I've been driving ever since!

Chapter 3 – Saturday Mornings

I was leisurely riding my horse down the trail, early one Saturday morning, and it was about 7:00 a.m. in 1956. Suddenly, I saw a bunch of riders racing across the screen and shots rang out!

I looked to my right, and this guy was approaching quickly on his horse. He shot his six-gun, and down I went hard. As I rolled to a stop, I aimed and shot. The rider fell from his horse and landed on top of me. We struggled, but I won in the end. We both climbed back on our horses, and off we went again.

The arm of the couch worked great as a horse, and Dad's belt was excellent for the reins. Of course, my horse was superior to my brother's, because I was two-and-a-half years older.

Again we rode down the trail watching Saturday morning westerns. Six Gun Theater and several others kept us entertained every Saturday morning while our folks were still asleep. Whenever the action on television increased, so did the action between my brother and me.

We were continually falling to the center of the couch, fighting or pulling our cap pistols to shoot the other one out of the saddle. I think this is what got us both started on wanting to be "cowboys" when we grew up.

Chuck in the yard at our duplex on Harding St.
North Long Beach
1954

As we got older the desire never left us. My grandfather always had a small acreage and a horse. We learned to ride at a very early age.

We used to go to Knott's Berry Farm in the evenings. The park would close at 6:00 p.m. during the winter months, but you could hang out in "Ghost Town" until 9:00. Hardly anyone was there, and the smell of the old buildings was intoxicating.

It was dimly lit, and we would go back into the 1880s! Several times, the best times, were to be there at night while it was raining. So very cool! Nobody was around, and we'd go into the general store and sit by the potbelly stove. Driving home I'd put on the Eagles "Desperado" tape, and that only added to the effect.

Melissa and I started traveling the west when I bought my VW bus: The Sierras, Colorado, Wyoming and Montana. Ghost towns and old mines were great country to see and be in.

One night Melissa and I had spent the day in Virginia City, Montana, a really cool old ghost town, away from everything.

We decided to spend the night in our bus, parked on the street near the end of town. An old saloon was across the street, and we had our first legal beer there; drinking age in Montana was 19. This saloon had been there since the 1880's. It still had the old bar and back bar inside and an old player piano.

As we climbed into our bed in the bus we could hear the piano playing this old time music, and this was going to serenade us to sleep. It was like being in 1880.

An hour or so later, still listening to the piano, we heard horses coming in down the street. We opened the curtains of our bus to see four cowboys riding down the street. They stopped in front of the saloon and tied up their horses.

This was too cool, so we got back up and headed back to the saloon. One of them was sitting on a bench out front and invited us to join him. He had a pillowcase that was full of peanuts and offered some to us. I went in and bought a couple of beers, and we sat out there eating peanuts, drinking beer and talking to the cowboys.

They worked on a large ranch nearby and had just ridden in for a couple of beers. They couldn't have been nicer, and we spent a couple more hours there at the saloon.

Chapter 4 -- Christmas 1960

My brother and I knew what we wanted for Christmas that year. The TV commercials of 1960 left us both wanting the battleship "Fighting Lady" and the "Whirlybird" helicopter. Both were large battery-operated toys, about 30" long. They both came with lots of extra accessories, and we knew that they would provide us with hours of fun.

We both put them on the top of our "lists" to Santa. Mom always had a plan to make us think that we wouldn't get the things we wanted most. They were either too expensive or Santa has to think of all the other "kids," so that our surprise on Christmas morning would be even greater. We continued to fall for this year after year.

Well, a couple of weeks before Christmas, Chris and I accompanied Mom to Cal Store. Our neighbor's car was in the shop, and she needed to go shopping, so Mom agreed to take her with us.

Once in Cal Store, my brother and I headed off to the toy department to check out the toys. After a time, Mom and our neighbor approached with a shopping basket full of Christmas gifts.

"Mom, here are the toys Chris and I want for Christmas, the Fighting Lady and the Whirlybird." Mom thought that they were pretty cool, but didn't tip her hand. Our neighbor then spoke up and asked Chris and I to each grab one because she was going to buy them for her nephews, since we thought that they would be such great gifts.

Chris and I were pretty excited as we left Cal Store carrying the toys that we wanted most. At least someone was getting them, and I was carrying them out to the car. No more was spoken about those toys or our neighbor's shopping trip.

After Chris and I had another sleepless Christmas Eve, Christmas morning had finally arrived. As the four of us entered the living room, there in front of the tree were two "Fighting Lady" battleships and two "Whirlybird" helicopters. Santa had come through for us. Those turned out to be great toys, giving Chris and I hours and hours of fun and enjoyment.

I later found out that these were the ones that we had carried out of Cal Store several weeks before Christmas. Mom had tricked us again!

Chapter 5 -- My Buddy Don

I met Don in Mrs. Roland's second grade class at Los Cerritos in the fall of 1958. He was fun to play with, and, as it turned out, he lived 14 houses from me. We ended up carpooling in second grade, and then in third grade we did the 1.3-mile walk on foot. My other neighborhood friends, the Skeber's, would also walk with us to and from Los Cerritos. In third grade, Mrs. Hunter's class, we began to play baseball in the Kiwanis T-Shirt League, and Don's Father was the coach. Our team was the Browns.

Don's Dad was a champion pole vaulter from his home state of Kansas, and he would spend a lot of extra time with Don and me in their front yard teaching us to throw, field and catch. Don also had a brother who was my brother's age and an older sister.

This was great for spending the night together. If Don and I made plans, our brothers would get together at the other's house. It was always more fun for me to stay at Don's. If his sister was not home, we would go into her room to hang out.

She had all the walls in her room covered with pictures from Teen Magazines of Elvis, Ricky Nelson and all the other rock and roll heartthrobs of the day. She also had her own record player and the largest collection of 45s that I had ever seen. It must have been hundreds.

We'd spend as much time as we could in her room listening

to records and thinking we were older than we really were. Don and I both attended Call's for two years learning square dance and then ballroom. (Forced by our Moms, because neither of us wanted to be there.)

In our neighborhood, we always had a minimum of five kids so we always had enough to play basketball, over-the-line, wiffle ball, hide and seek, ditch 'um and anything else we could think of to do. When we played sports, it was always Rich and I against Don, Mike and Bob. Rich and I always won.

Once we were playing a game of basketball down at the park, and Don and I got into a fight. Not wanting to hurt my friend, Don took several punches at me, and I grabbed him and tossed him to the ground. I then grabbed a hold of his shirt, held him over my knee and gave him several swats on the ass. That ended the scuffle.

As we got older, Don and I went to the movies a lot. At first it was Saturday matinees at the Towne and Crest. Later, it was almost every weekend, Friday or Saturday nights, at the movies.

Summers were a lot of fun. We both had parents that would give us money, and we'd walk to Red Fox Lanes and bowl three or four games and then spend the rest of our time playing arcade games. We once had a baseball arcade game going our way, and we amassed a large number of replays. Several other kids began to hang around watching, and we let them use some of the replays that we had on the game. This game was a dime to play, and this one older kid told us that the games at the Pike were only a nickel.

Neither one of us was allowed to go to the Pike. We were in fifth or sixth grade at the time, but the following week, instead of walking to Red Fox Lanes to bowl, we walked to the bus stop at Long Beach Blvd. and Del Amo and took the bus to the Pike.

We rode the Cyclone Racer that day, looked in the windows

of a tattoo parlor and played arcade games. The kid was right, the games were only a nickel, but they seemed to be older and in bad shape. After we rode the bus back to our neighborhood, we thought that we really did something adventurous. We couldn't wait to tell the other guys!

Don's mother was a tall beautiful woman. I always liked hanging out at their house and sneaking a glance her way. But in seventh grade she passed away suddenly, and Don and his brother found it difficult to cope.

By the time we started ninth grade, Don and I were starting to hang with different groups. By the time we started Poly, our contact became less and less, and Don stopped playing in our neighborhood football games. Luckily we expanded our neighborhood and several others soon became regulars in our games. It was still Rich and I against the rest.

Chris and I with Santa at Buffums

Chapter 6 – "Rio Bravo"

It's no secret that I have always loved westerns. I've been watching them since I was about five years old. I think I've seen them all! Probably missed a few, but who knows.

The first western I saw in a theater was "Shane." We were living in Elsinore for a short time, and Mom, Dad, Chris and I went to the walk-in theater in downtown Elsinore, maybe 1956 or '57.

This movie stands out in my mind because our dog Taffy had a litter of puppies six weeks earlier. Chris and I were both allowed to keep one. My brother chose the black one with curly hair and named him "Sammy." I chose a black one that had a half-white head. I called him "Petie" after the dog on "The Little Rascals."

When we drove up our dirt road, the dogs would race after our car, usually stopping at the paved highway road and then turning back towards the house. The night we went to see "Shane," the dogs followed us, and I watched them out the back window run on to the highway pavement.

As we gained speed on the highway I saw a car hit my dog "Petie." I hollered to Mom and Dad that I thought a car had hit Petie!

"No," they said. "Petie was fine." Waking up the next morning, there was no Petie! Petie was gone.

In 1959 the movie "Rio Bravo" was released. There was much excitement in the Mosley household about this, and we couldn't wait to see it.

We all loved John Wayne. Mom was a huge Dean Martin fan,

and two of our favorite shows were "Wagon Train" with Ward Bond and "The Real McCoy's" with Walter Brennan.

But the special star I couldn't wait to see was Ricky Nelson. I loved "Ozzie and Harriet," and Ricky was my favorite! And now he was going to be in a western with John Wayne. I just couldn't wait to see it!

We planned on going to see it on Friday night when Dad got home. It was playing at the Long Beach Drive-in. Friday was here, and Dad wasn't home from work. Time to leave was approaching, and Mom tried to call Dad at his shop. No one answered. Mom finally grabbed a blanket and some pillows and the three of us piled into our '59 Ford Galaxy and we headed off.

We stopped at Mrs. Chapman's Donuts on Santa Fe Avenue, as we always did and mom purchased a dozen donuts. We liked chocolate, but what we all loved the best were the plain cake donuts, and these were still warm!

Well, I loved every minute of this movie, and the music was perfect! The next morning, Saturday, I was the first one awake, as usual. I checked into my parent's room and Mom and Dad were in bed asleep. Life seemed good.

Later that afternoon I was telling Dad about the movie, how good it was and that he needed to see it. Dad later announced that we would go and see it tonight! I couldn't believe the news: Going to the drive-in two nights in a row. Well, later that night we repeated the events of the evening before with pillows, blankets and doughnuts.

Several years later as I began to identify the fact that my Dad was an alcoholic, I think back on the movie "Rio Bravo." For years I thought back on that Friday night we went to see it, only the three of us, and wondered if the drinking that Dean Martin portrayed in the movie was the beginning of Dad's drinking problem.

I watched "Rio Bravo" last night, maybe for the hundredth time. It's not the best western I have seen, but I always have to watch it when it's on; and it seems I always enjoy it!

Chapter 7 – Christmas '62

A few weeks before Christmas 1962, Mom and Dad had taken Chris and me to Dooley's for some shopping. In the toy department I discovered a red go-cart on display. Wow, this was really cool. Dragging Mom and Dad over to look at it before we left for home, I couldn't contain my enthusiasm for how much I wanted one for Christmas.

"Well, I don't think Santa can bring you something this large this year," Mom told me. So my brother and I accepted the fact that we weren't likely to get a go-cart this year.

As Christmas approached and school ended for vacation, I kept refining my list by watching all the commercials on television, as well as spending hours thumbing through the Sears catalogue.

Dad was coming home from work and spending his evenings locked away in the garage. I don't remember what we were told Dad was doing out there, but we were not to go out there! My parents were pretty good at hiding things from us, so I didn't give it much thought. I'm sure I bought into whatever they told us.

My brother and I were allowed to open one present every Christmas Eve, usually something from a grandparent, and the rest were to be opened Christmas morning after "Santa" had come. Chris and I could hardly sleep Christmas Eves in anticipation of the following morning.

We had to go and wake up our parents before going into the living room and checking out what Santa had left under the tree. This was usually a long and difficult proposition, as Mom and Dad were not early risers, and Christmas usually found Chris and me trying to get them out of bed around 5:30 a.m.

Well, this morning was different, they both climbed out of bed without any resistance. Mom said to wait so she could turn on the Christmas lights, and then she hollered to come on in.

Chris and I ran down the hall and stepped into the living room. There in front of the tree, and taking up half the living room, were two shiny red go-carts, the same ones we had seen at Dooley's several weeks before. We each jumped into the seat of one, and it wasn't long before my brother and I were arguing over which was which.

Dad had already figured this might happen, so he informed us that the one with the plaid seat was Chris' and the yellow seat was mine. It turned out that the brake and gas pedals were adjustable for taller and shorter kids, and Santa had already adjusted them for us.

Man, we wanted to take them out and run them up and down the street. After being told it was way too early, I think we started them out on the sidewalk at about 7:15. As we raced them up and down Pasadena Avenue several of our friends came running out to get their ride. Not long after the presents were all opened and Mom had fed us breakfast, Dad loaded the two carts into the back of our Ford wagon and took us up the street to the Bixby Knolls shopping center.

Between the Safeway store and TG & Y was a very large and pretty much unused parking lot. This turned out to be a great place for us to race around and not worry about cars and neighbors.

I later found out that these carts came unassembled, and Dad had spent those nights in the garage putting them together.

My Uncle Ronnie had a 1960 Ford Ranchero and would often come by and load up the go-carts and take us up to the parking lot. Unfortunately, after several months we wanted to go faster. A few unsupervised runs through Scherer Park were fun, but before the next Christmas we had sold them, hoping to get faster ones in the future.

Chapter 8 -- Scherer Park

My Parents moved us from Elsinore to Bixby Knolls in 1958 after nine months in the country. They purchased our house at 4562 Pasadena Ave., just a couple of houses from the soon-to-be-built Scherer Park.

Not long after we were settled, my brother and I went to play in the fields. Running down an embankment to a small creek, my brother fell head-first hitting his head on a rock and splitting open his forehead. That was the last time I remember playing there until the park was finished about a year later.

As kids the new park was great. It was huge and had a series of ponds, waterfalls, a flowing creek and small bridges. We would play cowboys and Indians, catch pollywogs, frogs and crawdads. It was also great for playing hide and seek and ditch'um!

The big hills and sidewalks were great once we started riding skateboards ("skobos") and flying kites. About the time we were in 5th and 6th grade there was always a game going on. The older boys in the neighborhood usually allowed me to participate in their games, as I was pretty good and larger than the others my age. It wasn't long before the park became ours!

After school and all summer long we played sports. We'd play basketball, baseball, over the line, softball; but more than anything we played football. We'd play flag, tackle, and touch. As we got older and larger we started playing two-hand touch, anywhere on the body! If you were mad at someone, you could really drill them, and they would go flying, but didn't really get hurt.

Once while we were in high school, we went to play, and there was someone on our field! Northtowners! They had eight players, as did we, and they challenged us to a game. They wanted to play tackle; we tried to talk them into our style of touch.

After they threw insults about how "soft" we were, we accepted the challenge of a game of tackle! I don't think they scored more than a touchdown against us as we ran up and down the field scoring at will. Rich was rolling out and throwing pass after pass to me and the others. We tackled hard and often and after several of them were hurting, they asked if we could change the game to "touch."

My buddy Rich seldom got mad, but one of the guys on their team, the one with the big mouth, had really pissed off Rich. "No, we are going to keep playing tackle!" Rich insisted.

Well, the game got ugly after that, and they walked off the field 20 minutes later, the "big mouth kid" bleeding from his left ear!

I once had a fight in the park, we drank at the park, but mostly we had a "blast" at the park!

Chapter 9 – Skobo

Living at the bottom of a hill in Bixby Knolls, my friends and I were always looking for new ways to have fun. We came down the hill on bicycles, wagons, scooters, Flex-Flyers and roller skates. One of Rich's friends had attached a board (1x6) across a roller skate, sat on it and glided his way down the street. Rich said that another of his friends took the skate apart and nailed it to a 2x4 and then he road it like a scooter. This sounded like fun and the two of us couldn't wait to try this. Rich said his friend called it a "scobo."

It was summer and I was usually the first one up in my house. As the sun was coming up I made my way out to the garage with my roller skates in hand. I began searching for the right board, saw and nails. As I began sawing a board to a length that I thought would be appropriate, I was startled by a voice. Looking up, standing in front of me in his white shirt and pants was our milkman. He had just dropped off our metal basket at the backdoor with Mom's order, milk, eggs and butter.

"What are you building?"

"I'm trying to build a skobo with my roller skate." As he looked at my "building supplies" and tools, he asked, "Want a hand"?

"Sure," I replied as he began looking around the garage for

another board. He found a 1x6, cut it with Dad's handsaw and quickly nailed it to my skate. I tried to explain that I was making a skobo to ride standing up, but he said all the boys were riding them sitting down, and he proceeded to nail it together. As he ponded in the last nail he told me to give that a try and then headed toward the front of the house and his milk truck.

I sat on the board, now attached to my skate, and coasted down the driveway toward the street. I found this not so much fun and not what I was trying to build.

I walked back to the garage as the morning dew was starting to burn off. I loved this time in the morning.

I grabbed the saw and went back to sawing my original piece of 2x4. Once I finished the cut, I took my other skate apart and laid both pieces of my skate on the 2x4. I had to find more nails. Searching Dad's workbench and toolbox, I finally found more nails that I could use. I nailed the skate on to the board, half of it to the front and the other half at the back of the 2x4. Success -- I now had a skobo.

I spent the next half hour riding down the driveway, practicing the art of the skobo.

I went back in the house, poured a small mixing bowl with cereal and ate breakfast. I then went to my room, removed my pajama bottoms and pulled on a pair of cut-offs, a clean t-shirt and went to the backdoor and grabbed my new skobo.

I decided to only go halfway up the street so as not to get going too fast my first try. I placed the skobo on the sidewalk with my right foot on it and then pushed off with my left. I was off! I made it past maybe two houses and then jumped off. The skate on the front was loose and it made me turn into the grass.

Back to the garage and re-nailed the skates. Back to the front yard and again it drifted sideways. I decided to wait until dad could give me a hand.

On Saturday Dad and I went out to the garage where he removed both skates and then attached them with wood screws and showed me the importance of aligning the skates so it would track straight. Dad also helped my friend Rich and his brother Bob with their skobos, and soon we could ride them all the way down the hill.

Later that summer I found a skateboard that I liked at Brownie's Toy store. It appeared to be perfect, but in large blue letters it said "Bun Busters." I bought the skateboard after several visits and then rode it home from the shopping center. It was so smooth, but after arriving home I took it straight into the garage, found a couple pieces of sandpaper and proceeded to sand off the big blue letters!

No "Bun Buster" on my skateboard!

Chapter 10 -- Summers in Bixby Knolls

In the early '60s summertime was the best! I usually was the second one up at my house. My Dad would wake up first, brew his coffee in the kitchen while playing my Marty Robbins "El Paso" album on the high-fi.

I usually got up as he was headed out the door to work. The first thing I would do was go to the kitchen and make a mixing bowl of Cherrios or Rice Krispies. I liked to eat my cereal out on the front porch, so quiet there, and I liked feeling the dew burn off while smelling the "night blooming jasmine."

After I finished, I would take my bowl to the kitchen, drop it in the sink, grab my baseball cards and head back out to the porch. I would flip through them, organize them into teams and decide which ones I wanted to trade.

Usually about this time one of my friends would be headed down the street, baseball cards in hand and the trading would begin. This normally would last an hour or so, and then it would be, what shall we do today?

"Over-the-line" at the park was a typical conclusion! I'll go get Rich and Bob, you go get Mike and Jon, and I'll call Don! After twenty minutes or so we were gathered and headed to the park. We loved playing over-the-line and played it for years.

Occasionally, there would be a couple of others at the park playing catch, and we would add them to the game. Our games were often 2 or 3-hour affairs, based on how competitive today's game was or how hungry we got. We would head our separate ways for lunch with a plan of meeting at someone's house after lunch.

Matinees at the Towne or Crest were always-good options, or bowling at Red Fox Lanes, but these always involved all of us being successful at coming up with money from our parents. Not always easy!

So typically we would just head up to the "shopping center." We'd walk up the front side, going into Brownie's Toy Store, walk through Grant's and Von's and then end up at Thrifty's. We'd buy candy or ice cream, look for change in the phone booths and then walk on the backside of the stores and head back home.

Afternoons might include riding our bikes, playing "pickle" in someone's yard, skate boarding down our hill or playing whiffle ball in the street!

As night approached, the group usually got smaller. "Do you want to spend the night?" After dinner we might play ditch 'um, ring doorbells and run, or just stay in eating popcorn and playing board games. Some parents would let us stay up and watch a scary movie or "The Steve Allen Show."

Life was good...

Chapter 11 -- Bixby Knolls Shopping Center

I grew up a couple of blocks from the Bixby Knolls Shopping Center during the '60s. When I was younger, my Mom would take my brother and me there to do our back-to-school shopping. Jeans, shirts and underwear from Anthony's, and then we'd go to lunch in the basement of Grants. We usually had tuna sandwiches with fries and chocolate malts. My Mom and brother really liked to dip their fries in their malts, but I preferred ketchup.

At Christmas Mom again took us there so we could get our shopping done. In 4th grade several students in my class brought to school their new box of 64 Crayola crayons with a sharpener, and I had to have them.

My Mom wouldn't buy them for me and said that I needed to do chores around the house to earn money and buy them myself. Anxious to get them, I had my Mom give me a list of what I could do to earn the money. I chose the lawn work and before long I raised a $1.25. Mom let me walk up to Grants by myself, and after paying the $1.04 for my Crayons, I walked to Brownie's Toy store a couple of doors down and bought baseball cards with my leftover change! It was a great day!

By the time I was in 6th grade, school shopping was Levi's from Anthony's, several shirts from Dunn's Men's Shop and then a trip to Penney's in Lakewood to get white t-shirts and underwear. My bucks and red socks came from Bundy Fox.

The guys in the neighborhood and I would spend plenty of time at the shopping center during the summer. TG&Y for candy, Brownie's Toy store, a walk through Grant's and then all the way up the block to Thrifty's for an ice cream. We were always keeping our eye out for girls that we might know from school.

If I had any money in my pocket I would buy a dozen crumb "dunkettes" from the lady at the Van de Kamp bakery at the front door of Vons. Once on our walk to the shopping center, I saw two dimes on the sidewalk on 45th street. I bent down to pick them up and there in the grass were another 6 or 7 dimes! This was a great day!

On occasion my parents would drive up to the rear door at Von's and Mom would run in and buy us chili dogs and root beer floats from the fountain.

In 7th grade I wanted some alone time and wanted to be an independent teenager. I started bugging my parents to let me go to a restaurant for dinner by myself. They finally relented and it was decided that I could walk to Thrifty's and have dinner by myself. So I put on my Pendleton shirt and armed with a couple of dollars, I walked to Thrifty's.

I sat at the counter and ordered my favorite dinner, burger, fries and a dinner salad with 1000 Island dressing. Waiting for my salad to come, I placed a quarter in the jukebox in front of me on the counter and made my selections. I thought that this was terrific!

After I finished eating, paid my check and remembered to leave a tip, I spent at least twenty minutes looking at magazines, not ready to go home yet. I remember that I purchased a copy of Sport Magazine with Sandy Koufax on the cover. It was a great night!

Chapter 12 – Donut Man

We were very lucky growing up in my neighborhood. Bixby Knolls shopping center was just up the street, Scherer Park three doors down and the Towne and Crest Theaters just a couple of blocks away.

But one of the greatest things when I was growing up was the Ice Cream Man and the Donut Man that circled our neighborhood on a regular basis.

"Good Humor" was the name of the Ice Cream Man's truck. I liked it when he came around on hot summer Days. I would usually buy a 50/50 bar or a Big Stick if I had a dime. It was a good treat on a hot summer afternoon. But it didn't hold a candle to the Donut Man.

We had two different donut trucks traveling up and down the streets of our neighborhood.

One was "The Golden Crust Bakery" and the other was "The Helms Man" as I called him. The Golden Crust truck eventually stopped coming around in the mid-sixties, and I was fine with that. His "stuff" wasn't as good as the Helm's Man, and he wasn't as friendly as the Helms Man either. Plus the Helms donuts were so much better.

I loved their "jelly donuts" the best, but they were more expensive than the glazed donuts, maybe 7 cents, and glazed were only a nickel.

As a growing boy of 9 or 10, I was always hungry. I would stop the "Donut Man" any time I had a nickel in my pocket.

Mom bought bread, cookies and occasionally donuts from him, however, usually she needed to be out of bread for her to come out of the house for a look in those long drawers of his truck.

I once had fifty cents when the Helms truck turned the corner and headed up our street. I waved him down and proceeded to buy a half dozen glazed donuts and one jelly donut. I sat on the steps of our house and quickly devoured the jelly donut and then one of the glazed.

I took the other five in the white bag into the kitchen where Mom was cooking dinner. I opened up a cabinet full of plates and placed my bag inside and closed the door quickly.

Mom asked what I was up to, and I explained I had bought donuts with my own money and was hiding them in the kitchen cabinet!

I was very surprised when Mom told me I couldn't hide my donuts, that I was to share with the rest of the family. A donut and glass of milk would make a great snack after dinner!

I was shocked and not very happy as my pleading fell on deaf ears. After dinner that evening, I watched my donuts disappear quickly while we set in the living room watching TV.

I was OK with sharing, but I had purchased the donuts with my own money, and had a two-day supply of donuts, or so I thought! When would I have another fifty cents that could go for donuts and not for baseball cards?

Several weeks later after a visit from Grandma Katie, I had a dollar, four quarters, "ice cream" money as Grandma called it.

The next day brought excitement as I tried to decide what to get with my "ice cream" money. After an hour or so, I had made up my mind.

I asked Mom if I could walk up to the "shopping center" and buy some baseball cards with my money from Grandma.

After the usual lecture of being careful when crossing Atlantic and using my "best manners" at Brownies Toy Store, I headed out the door. I purchased 10 packs of baseball cards and came home with 48 cents after tax.

I told mom that I was home and that I spent my dollar on baseball cards and then sat on the porch sorting my new cards with the others in my collection. But I was also waiting to hear the whistle of the Helms truck coming my way. Hopefully Mom wouldn't see him stop out front.

When I heard his approaching whistle, he stopped just around the corner as a neighbor lady had waved him down! Perfect, I thought, and ran around the corner to the stopped truck. Waiting for the neighbor lady to finish up, I stood patiently with forty-eight cents in my pocket.

"Can I help you," asked the Donut Man.

"Could I see the donuts?" I said.

As he pulled open the long drawer of donuts, I was trying to decide if I wanted jelly, glazed or a combination of the two. I decided to buy all glazed; yep six glazed donuts. He placed them in the white bag and walked slowly back towards the house, eating one as I decided what I'd do with the rest.

I could place them in the kitchen and share them with the family, eat them all right now, or I could hide them in my bedroom.

Yep, I would hide them in my bottom dresser drawer.

I made them last three days, only eating two a day!

This became my new hiding place for donuts that I didn't want to share, although it was rare that I had enough money to buy enough donuts to hide. Usually I only bought a couple at a time, and I would eat them before I made it back into the house!

Chapter 13 -- The Grey Ghost or The Knight

In the early '60s my world revolved around my neighborhood and the friends that lived there. We lived on Pasadena Avenue between 45th & 46th Streets. The streets in this area are hilly. 45th is the top and Pasadena drops steeply down to 46th street and into Scherer Park. It was the perfect neighborhood to grow up in.

Our gang consisted of Don Kirkpatrick, Rich and Bob Skeber, Mike Derbyshire and me. We all had brothers a couple of years younger if we needed someone else to torment.

So, the hill always was something to conquer! Riding bikes down the hill as fast as we could and setting up a board on a cinder block was often fun.

Making our own skobos from roller skates and 2x4s was always a challenge for the hill. The skobos tended not to want to go straight the faster we went. Nevertheless, we got pretty darn good!

Then came store-bought skateboards! This made us go faster and straighter, so it didn't take too long to master the hill, and we needed another challenge.

Up near the top of the hill the neighbors were gone for

several weeks, and we found the next challenge: running our skateboards all the way across their lawn once we picked up enough speed, coming out of their neighbor's driveway and then racing all the way down the hill!

This was so much fun, in fact, that by the time they returned home, we had worn a dirt path all the way across their front lawn. We were punished somehow for that, but I'm not sure what the punishment was.

So Rich had a secret project going on in his garage. "Top secret," he told me. Well, one afternoon he was ready to unveil the project to me. So, into the garage he takes me, and there in front of me is this pretty cool soapbox derby car that he's been building. The bottom was made of 2x4s with the wheels and axles taken from a wagon. The body was made out of plywood, and the front axle was attached to another 2x4 that had a rope going through drilled holes near each front wheel. This was the steering mechanism.

The whole thing was painted grey. "Why paint it grey?" I asked. "The only paint I could find in the garage," was his answer. It looked pretty cool!

"Is it ready to run?" I wanted to know. "No, I think I want to name it."

So we spent the rest of the afternoon trying to come up with a cool name. I thought, when I went home to dinner that it was going to be called the "Grey Ghost."

The next afternoon Rich brought the Grey Ghost out into his front yard. As I headed up the street to his house I hoped this was going to be the maiden voyage.

When I got there, he had a painted an outline of a knight on the hood of the soapbox derby car with "the Knight" hand painted across the top of the hood.

"I'm ready to try it out," says Rich. So we slowly used the rope to pull it up to the top of the street. Rich then climbed into "the Knight" as I held it so it wouldn't roll. As I'm holding it, Rich pulled the rope back and forth. It appeared he would be able to turn it.

"Ok, give me a push" -- and off he goes on the maiden voyage of the Knight! Running behind him, as it picks up speed, my thought is, I want to be next!

Well, Rich gets about half way down the hill, which is about where his house is. Suddenly, he veers left at almost a right angle to the street and BAM -- right into the curb.

Well, the Knight stopped immediately upon impact with the curb. The "grille" went flying as his feet and legs pushed it out the front. And as his body continued moving forward, the whole body of the car got torn off and ended up wrapped around Rich who was now about 4 feet in front of the Knight!

"Why didn't you use the brake?" I yelled as I come running up to the destroyed vehicle. Rich gave me that sly grin that he had and told me, "Didn't have a brake!"

We spent the next ten minutes sitting on the sidewalk, laughing at the remains of the Knight, with Rich recanting the tale of the maiden run -- and then demise of vehicle! We took the pile of splintered grey wood and bent front wheels back to his garage.

"What if we drill a hole in this hardball and tie it to the end of a 20 foot piece of rope," he said. Then one of us could swing it around and the other could hit it with a bat. We'll get batting practice, and we won't have to chase it!!

Chapter 14 -- The Pigeon

Living close to the Bixby Knolls Shopping center, we went there a lot. As kids we liked to hang out there, shopping for baseball cards, toys, records, clothes, ice cream, magazines and looking at girls. This shopping center had it all.

Mom always did the grocery shopping at Vons and occasionally she would bring home chilidogs from the snack bar at the back entrance. On one such occasion Mom went to pick up a few items at Vons and told us she would bring home chilidogs for dinner.

My brother and I were thrilled, hungry and couldn't wait for her to get home. As an eleven-year-old I was always hungry! What made these chilidogs so good was that the lady placed mayonnaise, mustard, ketchup and hamburger relish on the hotdogs, and then piled on the chili, with a lot of cheese on top. I still make my chilidogs the same way today.

As Mom pulled into the driveway, Chris and I rushed out to grab groceries and the food so we could sit down and eat sooner. As I approached our Ford station wagon I saw something moving at the front of the car. As I looked closer there was a pigeon stuck in the grille of the car, one wing free and flapping back and forth. I yelled at Mom to come look as I began to free him from the car grille. As he came loose, I placed him on our driveway, and he tried to fly but couldn't. His right wing had been stuck in the grille and was just hanging. It appeared to be broken.

Mom said to pick him up and bring him into the house. After placing him on the bathroom sink, Mom sent me to grab a sock out of my drawer. With a pair of scissors she cut off the toe of the sock and slipped it over the pigeon. It looked like it would hold the wing in place, so she removed it and cut holes for its legs. Slipping the sock back over the bird, Mom said, "Take it out into the backyard and place him out on the grass." Watching the pigeon head into the bushes we felt that it might be OK. Chris came outside with a piece of bread, ripping it into tiny pieces and scattering it near the flowerbed!

Finally sitting down to eat, the chilidogs were cold, but the excitement of having our very own pigeon seemed to make them taste fine.

For the next couple of months we fed and held the pigeon in the backyard. Mom finally convinced us that we should remove the sock and see if its wing had healed.

My brother and I were reluctant, as we figured it might fly away. But Mom always seemed to know best, so we removed the sock and set the pigeon on the grass. He seemed to be healed. He could hold the wing in place just like the other one. Expecting it to fly away, it just hopped over to a small piece of bread that was lying in the grass, and made no attempt to fly away.

Chris and I continued to feed our pigeon bread and dry cereal along with some parakeet food for the next week. We figured that he liked it here and was going to stick around. However, one afternoon our pigeon was gone! My brother was pretty upset, so Mom said let's get into the car and go get chilidogs.

As we drove through the parking lot at rear entrance to Vons, there was a group of 8 to 10 pigeons looking for food scraps near the backdoors. "There," Mom said to Chris, "There's our pigeon, back home where he belongs."

I asked her later was that really our pigeon? She said it didn't matter, your brother thought it was!

Chapter 15 -- Autograph?

Los Cerritos was a wonderful school. I started there in Mrs. Roland's second grade class, and I finished with Mr. Bamrick's sixth grade class in 1963. I can still smell the Eucalyptus trees in my mind. I have vivid memories from all my teachers and my classes.

In second grade spelling, we always had a "bonus" spelling word. After missing that word on several tests, I was determined to get it right the next week. As we wrote down our ten spelling words, Mrs. Roland wrote down the bonus word for the week. That word was "between."

I'm not sure why I remember this, but I was determined to get it right that week, so I studied it very hard. I was so proud after that spelling test, because I got all ten words plus the bonus word correct, and Mrs. Roland commented about my hard work that week at the top of my test paper.

Third grade was Mrs. Hunter, and we studied the Pueblo Indians and built a pueblo in class. I thought that was a really cool project. I also remember being called on to read out loud during English one day. About half way through the paragraph my eyes started watering, and I couldn't finish. Mrs. Hunter looked at my watery eyes and had someone else finish reading. That afternoon she gave me a note for my parents to have an eye examine, and weeks later I ended up with a pair of reading glasses.

Fourth grade was a really fun class with Mrs. Collins. I remember that the custodian would occasionally wheel into class a large black radio, and we would listen to special programming. "This is radio station KLON, the station of the Long Beach Public Schools." One of the girls used to buy records and bring them to school. Mrs. Collins would sometimes play them during "music" class. She brought Peter, Paul and Mary's "Puff the Magic Dragon", and the whole class sang along.

Another time she brought David Seville and the Chipmunks into class, and when she pulled it out of the album cover, the record was red vinyl! I had never seen a colored record before, and when I got home from school that day, I insisted to Mom that I had to get a copy.

The same girl Judy also brought to school the box of sixty-four Crayola crayons which included a sharpener in the box. This was another thing that I just had to have.

In fifth grade I had Mr. Howarth in a fifth-and-sixth grade combination class. My two best friends, Don and Rich, were in the class, Rich in sixth and Don in fifth with me. Among the other sixth graders I remember was Brad, who was always funny, Gary, who I thought was the "coolest" guy in school, and a girl named Delight who reminded me of Annette from the Mickey Mouse Club.

The best week of school that year was when the sixth graders went to camp, and we had a substitute all week. There were only a dozen or so fifth graders in class.

That year I had to have a pair of Levi's, a Pendleton shirt and a pair of "bucks," as well as a pair of "Purcell" blue tip tennis shoes. Oh yeah, and Penney's Towncraft t-shirts. Before this, brand names didn't matter much, but this year in the fifth-sixth combo, it was very important.

I used to go home from school that year and watch "Soupy Sales." As television was pretty limited back then, Channel 9 used to show the same movie every night of the week, "Million Dollar Movie."

I remember one week the movie was John Wayne in "She Wore a Yellow Ribbon." One day that week the cute girl Delight came to school wearing a yellow ribbon in her hair, and the sixth grade boys teased her about it. As the movie portrays, "She wore it for her true love who was in the Cavalry."

By the time I bought my second pair of Levi's, a felt belt was no longer "cool," and the guys were cutting off the belt loops. I asked my Mom if she could do this for me, and she didn't have time. So I took a pair of scissors and my Levi's to my room and cut them off myself.

When I was finished, I had cut holes at the top and bottom of each belt loop where the loops had been attached to the Levi's. In so doing I ruined my new pants, and Mom was not very happy. However, when she bought me another pair, she showed me how to use a seam ripper to remove all the stitching.

Sixth grade was the best! We were now the "Big Guys on Campus." I was student body vice president, audio/visual man (operated the projector at assemblies) and Mr. Bambrick was the best teacher I ever had.

At the beginning of school that year most of the guys played "kickball," before school, at recess and especially during lunch. We had decided that first day of school to keep track of everyone's homeruns.

It made it more fun, and I ended up winning the homerun title by a lot, with Lee and Greg, second and third, with fifth grader Steve and fourth grader Mikey not too far behind.

One day after lunch near the end of the school year, three boys from the third grade, who watched us play at lunch every day, came up and asked if they could have my autograph. No one has asked me since.

Chapter 16--6th Grade Student Faculty Game

I attended Los Cerritos Elementary School, which was a quiet elementary school in a quiet affluent neighborhood in Long Beach. It was at the end of San Antonio Drive in the Virginia Country Club neighborhood, just minutes from Rancho Los Cerritos, the original ranch house of Long Beach.

My sixth grade teacher was Mr. Bambrick. (He's one of three teachers that made a great impression on me growing up. The other two were Mr. Zielenski at Hughes and Coach Herbold at Poly.)

Sixth grade was cool because you were big man on campus. The Beach Boys and Jan & Dean were big in music. Kickball was terrific. I became the A/V tech and got to miss a little extra class time running the projector in the auditorium. I ran for and won class Vice President, but lost to a girl for class President during the second semester. Levis, bucks, Pendletons and Madras shirts were the dress. 6th grade camp was OK, not great, as everyone hoped for snow, but it didn't snow for us!

I came home from camp and my parents had bought a lot of

new furniture and things didn't feel right. It felt like I had been gone a long time, or maybe this really wasn't my house!

I had my first girlfriend in sixth grade. We were going steady, and I gave her a Saint Christopher medal, which was the custom at the time. But what I was really looking forward to was the student/faculty softball game the last week of school!

"Coachie" was great. She was in charge of the cafeteria as well as the playground, knew I loved the hamburgers in the cafeteria and would occasionally bring me an extra if some girl didn't want hers. I always set at the end of a table in the cafeteria and "Coachie" (Mrs. Hubbard) would always walk by and tell me to move my "violin cases" out of the aisle! I had big feet, what can I say?

Well, one day near the end of the school year, I was told to go the office. I could not figure out what I had done and was very nervous on the short walk to the office.

"Please go into Mr. Martin's office," I was told. I walked in and Mr. Martin and "Coachie" were waiting for me. Mr. Martin then asked if I would be the coach for the students in the big game next week: pick the players, make the line-up and hold a couple of practices.

Man, was I excited! So I picked the best team I could, held a couple practices after school and set the positions and line-up for the big game. What was really exciting for me was playing in front of the whole school! As the big game was about to start Mr. Martin started warming up, and damn, he could really sling the softball! Like, really fast! Turned out he played for the Long Beach Nighthawks. Well, now I wasn't as excited as we came to bat.

Some of the sixth grade girls, my girlfriend included, had dressed in red skirts, white blouses and had made red and white pompoms. They had been practicing also. They had routines and cheers, and this made the game even better! Well, we lost to the faculty that day, all because Mr. Martin showed us no mercy until the last inning, and we could only manage a few runs off of him.

As the game ended in our defeat, and as I said my goodbyes to everyone, I started my long walk home. As I walked out to the front of school there was my girlfriend! She ran up to me, handed me a pom-pom and told me how great I played! As I looked in her eyes and thanked her, I turned and started my walk home. After I was a couple of blocks from school, I said to myself, "I think she wanted to kiss me!"

I also thought, "Why didn't I walk her home?"

Too shy!

What an idiot!

I replayed that moment in my head all the way home!

Chapter 17 -- Drive or Fly

In the 6th or 7th grade, one of my good friends from school was Greg. His birthday was coming up, and I was invited to go surfing with him and his dad in Dana Point. They had a beach house there. So I was dropped off at his house on Friday afternoon, surfboard and clothes ready to go.

At dinner his dad asked if we wanted to fly or drive? The only small plane I'd flown in was the seaplane to Catalina, and I was really excited to fly! So, the plan was to go by plane.

The next morning we put our gear in the station wagon and headed to Compton. Instead of going straight to the airport we went to the "ranch." They had a ranch in the middle of Compton. Wow, it was pretty cool!

It was an old two-story farmhouse with a barn, a horse and corrals with lots of fruit trees. Greg's grandma lived there, and after being introduced to her, Greg and I headed out to explore.

Greg's dad had a little business to do before we could head out. On the other side of the ranch was their business, a large trucking company.

We explored the big old barn, shot the twenty-two and then decided to go and find his dad. I was amazed at all the trucks and some large cranes, but in particular was the biggest truck I had ever seen. You had to climb a steel ladder that was attached to the side to get up to the cab!

Greg's dad explained it was the largest street legal truck in the country and had been built to haul rockets from California to Cape Canaveral in Florida.

Well, before we headed to the airport Greg told his dad he wanted a new Hobie surfboard for his birthday.

"We'll have to drive then," we were told. I was a bit disappointed as we now headed south to Dana Point and the Hobie surf shop.

Greg picked out his new board, a wet suit and grabbed a couple surfer magazines to keep us occupied when not out in the water!

Their beach house was a really nice mobile home right on the sand! Very cool! We could grab our boards, walk across the sand and be in the water within a couple of minutes.

It also turned out that neither of us were very good surfers, only occasionally catching a wave and riding it all the way in.

But we had a blast.

Chapter 18 -- TV Night

My family loved watching westerns on television back in the late '50s and early '60s. *Maverick, Johnny Yuma, Lawman, Sugarfoot, Rawhide* and *Wagon Train* were our favorites.

But in 1962-63 we had a family tradition. On Thursday nights, we had TV Night.

It was a great family night of television shows. We'd watch *Father Knows Best, The Donna Reed Show, Leave It To Beaver, Ozzie and Harriet* and *The Real McCoys.*

The other special treat was that we ate on TV trays in the living room. It wasn't often that we didn't eat dinner in the dining room.

Mom didn't want to cook and do the dishes on TV Night, so on Thursday night TV dinners became a treat also. Occasionally we had TV dinners on other nights too, and we all thought they were good. But the best was when Dad brought home dinner.

His shop was on Lakewood Blvd., just south of Artesia. My favorite was when Dad stopped at the Bob's Big Boy on the corner of Lakewood and South St. I could eat a lot during this time in my life, so my order was always the same, the Big Boy Combo: a burger, fries and salad with 1000 Island dressing.

And then instead of dessert I'd have an extra Big Boy hamburger. It was so good!

When the family tired of Bob's, which I never did, Dad would stop by Fio Rito's on Paramount and bring home a large cheese pizza and a family-size order of spaghetti.

My brother and I would take our baths early and get into our pajamas by 6 o'clock and wait for Dad to pull into the driveway with our dinner. This was also the night that we could stay up until 9:30 on a school night!

My Mom's step Dad lived in Long Beach and was a milkman. During the early sixties, he came to dinner on Sundays. Mom usually went all out with a great home cooked meal. We ate at the dining room table, and Chris and I couldn't wait to be excused from the table.

The conversation with "Grandpa" was usually pretty boring. All he did was deliver milk everyday and then play golf in the afternoons. However, my ears perked up whenever he played golf with Dodger players Ed Roebuck and Stan Williams. I was a huge Dodger fan.

Then it was off to the living room for the *Wonderful World of Disney* and then *Ed Sullivan*. I always liked *Disney*, especially when he had *Davy Crockett* or *Zorro*. Ed Sullivan wasn't my favorite until The Beatles and other musical acts of the day were on. But it seemed like most of the time he had on *Topo Gigio*, which I hated!

As we got a little older we continued to watch programs together, but it was never as special as that one TV season...

Chapter 19 – The Saw

My Mom wanted to buy a "jig saw." I couldn't imagine why. I was in 5th grade at Los Cerritos and had just received a really cool clock radio for my birthday. It was brown and made from very hard plastic.

One Saturday afternoon Mom and Dad pulled into the driveway with a large item sticking out the trunk of our 1959 Ford Galaxy. Dad was backing the car up our driveway as Mom opened the gate that divided our front and backyards.

Untying the rope that held the trunk lid down, I can see the saw that Mom's been wanting. It was heavy, grey and had a very small blade. Dad and I slid the saw into the garage near an electrical outlet and Dad plugged it in. Mom came over with a scrap piece of wood and turned on the saw, made a couple of cuts and was now ready to go!

Over the next few weeks Mom spent a lot of time in the garage working on her project, and she and Dad were running back and forth to the hardware store.

Arriving home from school one afternoon and entering my bedroom, my brother and I both had new headboards adorning our twin beds. They looked really nice, stained a dark brown, with the shelf divided into three sections.

My sports magazines were to one side, baseball card

box on the other, and my clock radio in the center. My brother's headboard had his "monster" models spread out on his shelves.

Mom was right behind me as I checked them out and was waiting for my reaction!

"They are really great," I said. "Where did you get them?"

"This is what I've been building in the garage the last few weeks!"

I was really surprised that Mom could make something like these, and as nice as these turned out.

It was really neat having my clock radio just inches above my head. I could listen to music or the Dodger game ever night, and no one else could hear it. I would set my alarm to go off every morning for school, and I'd wake up to KRLA. Having my baseball cards right there was great as well!

I used this headboard for 4-5 years, until I was moved into a makeshift bedroom after Mom remarried and I was saddled with two stepsisters, as well as my own brother and sister.

I don't recall Mom ever building anything else with her saw. It sat idle in the garage for many years gathering dust in corner where Dad and I put it years earlier.

I think her second husband may have sold it when he took over the garage while I was in high school.

The two headboards were sold off at a garage sale in '71 when Mom was again alone and sold the house to move to Lakewood.

I still get a smile when I think of Mom in the garage building furniture!

Chapter 20 -- Towne Theater

I grew up in the neighborhood behind the Towne Theater from 1957 until October 1970. I spent a lot of time at Scherer Park, Bixby Knolls Shopping Center and the Towne and Crest Theaters.

We used to go to matinees during the summer, 35 cents, and then my friends and I would go on Friday and Saturday nights during the 7th, 8th and 9th grades.

My first date was in the 6th grade, and I took my girlfriend to the Towne. My first two years in organized baseball, the Kiwanis-T-Shirt league, we had our year-end banquets at the Towne Theater.

When I attended orientation at the Press-Telegram to become a paperboy, I won four free passes to the Towne Theater.

I remember seeing "The Seven Voyages of Sinbad" and "20,000 Leagues Under The Sea" with my friends, Rich and Bob Skeber at the Towne. I took my brother Chris to see "Toby Tyler," and he got so mad at me for calling him the main character "Toby Toilet" that he started crying!

I saw movies "Operation Petticoat," "Goldfinger," "Thunderball" and Doris Day movies with friends Mike Derbyshire and Don Kirkpatrick. Once Don and I were the first to buy tickets for "Lawrence of Arabia," and we hung out talking with friends from school until the movie was about to start and walked in to a nearly full theater. We ended up sitting in the far corner of the first row.

I once had a girl from Hughes call me to tell me that her friend Karen wanted to meet me at the Towne on Saturday afternoon, the day after we graduated 8th grade. I told her I had baseball practice and didn't think I would make it. On Saturday I decided to skip baseball and meet Karen at the theater. After walking there alone and buying a ticket, Karen, assuming that I wouldn't be there, didn't show up.

The first month of 9th grade, every Friday the kids from Hughes would meet at the Towne on Friday nights, and we would take up the entire 2nd and 3rd rows of seats. I met my next girlfriend in the 3rd row on one of those Friday nights.

We watched "horror" movies, romantic movies like "The Graduate," "Love Story" and "Romeo and Juliet." I watched with great excitement "Woodstock" and wished that I had been there!

Not long after "Woodstock" I watched the movie "Easy Rider" and half way thru the movie I couldn't wait to hit the open road. Forty-five minutes later I left the theater in silence and shock, as the two heroes are gunned down to end the movie.

On my third date with Melissa we went to the Towne and watched "The Thomas Crown Affair" with Steve McQueen and Faye Dunaway.

The Towne Theater was like my second home. I enjoyed going to the fancier Crest Theater, just down the street as well, but most of my childhood memories seemed to centered around the Towne Theater.

Chapter 21 -- The Slap

In the summer of 1963 I was 12 years old. I had just had my favorite school year, sixth grade at Los Cerritos, and I was anxiously anticipating the start of seventh grade at Hughes.

I had been going steady with Cynthia for most of the school year. We had gone on one date, a Saturday matinee at the Towne Theater, and we danced once at Greg's party. I hadn't called her since the end of school, almost a month earlier. Too shy I guess. But girls were usually on my mind, when not playing sports, of course.

My friend Don and I were hanging out at the Bixby Knolls Shopping Center, something that we often did, when coming toward us one day was our friend Mike with his new girlfriend Christy and another girl whom we had never seen before.

We met on the sidewalk in front of Anthony's, and Mike introduced us again to Christy and to the other girl, her friend Mickey. Mickey was pretty darn cute with short brown hair, and she seemed very talkative and friendly. We all walked up to Thrifty's, had an ice cream and continued to talk.

At one point Christy and Mickey wondered off together, and when they returned, Christy whispered in Mike's ear. As we started walking back towards the north end of the shopping center, Mike said he needed to talk with me.

At this point we were at 45th Street and started across Atlantic toward Don's house. While waiting for the light to change, Mike told me that they were going to Christy's house to play "spin the bottle," and Mickey wanted me to go too. She thought I was "cute."

As we stood in front of Don's house, Mickey took my hand, and Christy and Mike informed Don what our plans were and explained that we would see him later.

Don looked dejected as the four of us started walking away, hand in hand. As we reached the corner of Pasadena, Don walked up to the four of us and asked me, "I thought you were going steady with Cynthia?"

I was caught off guard and didn't know what to say. Christy asked me, "Is that true? You have a girlfriend?"

"Well, yes," I said, "but I haven't talked to her since summer started!"

Mickey let go of my hand, and all five of us continued walking up the street.

After walking several blocks, Christy told me, "Chuck, you need to leave. Don's coming with us now!"

Then I was feeling dejected as the four of them continued walking. However, I quickly caught back up with them, wanting to plead my case. I wanted to play spin the bottle with these two girls.

As I approached them I said, "Hey, wait a minute."

When they stopped and turned, Christy walked up to me and slapped me in the face! "Go home!" she said.

"Wow, what just happened?" I was thinking to myself. I turned and went home, bummed out for the rest of the day.

I didn't mind the slap, but not getting to play spin the bottle and knowing that that was what these guys were off doing was the painful part.

Well, about a week later Mom said, "Cynthia's on the phone."

Pulling the phone into my bedroom for privacy, I heard Cynthia say, "Someone wants to talk to you."

The phone is handed over, and I recognized the new voice immediately. It was Cynthia's friend Diane.

Diane told me, "Cynthia wants to break up with you since you haven't called her since school was out," and then she hung up the phone!

Looking back on all this, I was not bothered by the slap, didn't mind Cynthia breaking up with me, or that Don and Mickey went together all summer. But still, I never got to play "spin the bottle." That has bothered me the most!

Chapter 22-- Regrets

Regrets, I have a few, but then again too few to mention!

In 1965 I'm in the 8th grade at Hughes Junior High. One day I'm sitting in art class, and a girl gets permission to go to the restroom. As she walks by me she drops a note on my lap! This was the junior high girls' version of the Pony Express -- or the cell phone of today.

I read the note and it says, "Judy loves you!" Well, I knew whom she was talking about; I'd known her since the third grade. I really wasn't interested, but after class on my way to my locker, this small group of girls is verbally assaulting me with, “She loves you, call her, dance with her at the sock hop next Friday.”

Well, this goes on for a week: between every class these girls hound me! They were like a swarm of bees buzzing around me. One afternoon after school, I'm headed to my locker, exhausted from this banter, and who's at my locker, Judy!

She starts making small talk, asking silly questions as her girlfriends are now coming towards us. So, I decide to do the only thing I can think of to get out of this mess: I ask her to go steady!

Well, you would've thought she'd won the Lottery -- jumping up and down and then running down the hall yelling to her pack of girlfriends.

I headed out of there as quickly as I could, walking home by myself wondering what I had just done. What was I going to tell the guys? Geez, I couldn't tell them that I was going steady.

I was sick.

I didn't go out once I got home, but lay on the bed listening to the radio, feeling terrible and wondering what to do. It was agonizing!

I woke up the next morning not wanting to go to school, but my Mom wasn't buying any of my excuses. So I silently headed to school meeting the guys on the way, hardly saying a word.

When we got to school, I successfully hit my locker and headed to homeroom without seeing "her" or any of the crazies.

After homeroom, I'm headed to second period, and here she comes.

I'm sick to my stomach, and I don't have a plan. As she approaches, the first words out of her mouth are, "Did you mean what you said last night?"

Wow, I thought to myself, this is my opening.

"No," I told her," I didn't."

Well, off she went bawling down the hall. I felt like crap, but also very relieved. I was free!

I never spoke to her again, even though we continued on to Poly. She never came close to me again, which was OK, and the next few weeks at school her "girls" really gave me the cold shoulder. But this was definitely better than having them buzzing around me!

So, I've felt bad about hurting her feelings all these years. It's a regret I have, but I'm glad I was able to end it on the next day.

Oh, and the girl that dropped the note on my lap and started all this, calls me about a month later on a Friday night to let me know that "Karen" really likes me, and they are going to be at the Towne Theater tomorrow afternoon, and I should come...

Chuck Mosley
Hughes Jr. High
1965

Chuck Mosley
Hughes Jr. High
1966

Hughes Football 1966

front row l-r John Robinson, Chuck Mosley, Greg Burden, Bob Headley, Mike Lane, Craig Holmblad, Bond Nichols

back row l-r Greg Vanley, Bruce Ingram, Jim Lemon, Greg Vanley, Kurt Whiteman

Chapter 23 -- Vin Scully

In the fall of 1959, I watched my first baseball game on TV. I was eight years old and home sick with a cold. The Dodgers were playing the Chicago White Sox in the World Series. I was just getting interested in baseball, and my new friends up the street were teaching me to play. After watching the series, I was hooked.

In the spring of the next year, while shopping with my Mom at Ray and Eddies Market, I spotted baseball cards at the checkout stand, and I purchased my first pack for a nickel. My friends and I started playing catch, playing "pickle," collecting baseball cards and listening to the Dodger games on radio with our parents.

I soon realized that all the parents of my friends listened to the Dodgers on radio, especially enjoying the call of the game by Vin Scully. I remember some afternoons walking up the street to the Skeber's house and being able to hear Vinny all the way up the street! Everyone in the neighborhood it seemed had their radios tuned to the Dodgers.

In 1960 the Union 76 gas stations were giving away "The Dodger Family Albums," a short bio with pictures and stories of all our favorite Dodgers. I couldn't wait to pick up the newest one every week.

For my birthday in 1960, my parents took me to the Los Angeles Coliseum to see the Dodgers and the Cubs. As we walked out of the tunnel and saw the field for the first time, I was in awe at the field. The grass was so green. I remember that you could hear Vinny from anywhere in the stadium, as everywhere people had transistor radios tuned to the game. It was heaven!

Stan Williams pitched that night and the Dodgers won. I was officially addicted and talked my parents into trying to get a few autographs after the game. We went to the players' parking lot and waited. That evening I got the autographs of Maury Wills, Norm Larker and Wally Moon. My Dad left us and went to use the restroom and ran into Vin Scully. He said Vinny was really nice, but he couldn't get his autograph because I had the pen and paper!

I used to love when the Dodgers played in San Francisco because those were the only Dodger games televised back then. It was a big deal in my family. Three days of baseball bliss.

My Mom would make my Dad and me bologna sandwiches for the Sunday game, consisting of several pieces of bologna, soft white bread with mayonnaise and mustard, and I knew they were special because she would add lettuce and bring them to us on a plate with Bell Brand potato chips. It was the best!

I can't tell you how many Dodger games I've been to or how many times I fell asleep listening to the game. The constant for me has always been the voice of Vin Scully calling the games. I listened to the Dodger game last week, and Vinny sounded as good as ever!

While listening the other night a flood of memories came racing back through my mind. I guess I listened to more games during the '60s than at any other time.

I remember Juan Marichal hitting John Roseboro in the head with a bat, Sandy Koufax tossing his four no-hitters, Scully's great call of the ninth inning of Sandy's perfect game against the Cubs, Drysdale throwing high and tight to Mays, Maury Wills stealing 104 bases, Wally Moon and his "moonshots" at the Coliseum, Frank Howard and his long home runs, Garvey, Cey, Lopes and Russell, Tommy Lasorda, Orel Hershiser and Fernando mania!

Kirk Gibson's homerun in game one of the '88 World Series is still one of my favorites. I was at Dodger Stadium for several World Series games in both '77 and '78. While working overtime in construction, we often listened to Vinny call the Dodger games.

When I listen to Vinny, I don't know if I'm 10, 20, 30, 40, 50 or in my 60's. Time stands still!

I have always judged the fact that I'm not old as long as my Grandma was still living and Vince Scully was still announcing Dodger games.

Well, my Grandmother passed away several years ago at the age of one hundred, and this is Vince Scully's last year broadcasting the Dodgers.

As Vin Scully would say at the beginning of each Dodger broadcast,

"So pull up a chair. It's time for Dodger baseball."

Chapter 24 -- Golf

My Parents decided that they wanted to play golf. There was a driving range near our house on Long Beach Blvd. just north of the railroad tracks between Scherer Park and Dooley's Hardware store.

My Mom's step-dad was a milkman, so after his route he would go and play at Lakewood Country Club, as he would be finished delivering milk by 1:00 in the afternoon.

My Dad bought a used set of clubs from him and Mom bought a set of "beginners" clubs at the driving range pro shop.

They both began taking lessons in the evenings at the driving range and then go have dinner at Ken's or Lucy's.

This went on for several months and they decided to go and play the front nine at Lakewood Country Club late one Saturday afternoon.

My Grandma Katie had bought me a junior set of clubs, four irons and a putter in a small canvas golf bag. I had only been hitting wiffle balls in the backyard and Dad took me to the driving range one Sunday morning. I was about 10.

I talked my parents into letting me come with them, but I would have to stop if I could not keep up. I agreed.

On the first hole they hit fairly long tee shots, but they weren't very straight. I teed off and only drove the ball 50 to 75 yards, but my shots were straight as an arrow. As the afternoon continued, I could see the frustrations on their faces. Golf was not east.

After six holes they decided they were through for the day. I decided to tally up the score cards and I had beaten them both! They were proud of me, but I could tell that they were not very happy about their game.

Mom stopped playing not long after this, and Dad only went to the driving range occasionally. My Mom's step-father started giving him lessons.

A year or two later Dad asked if I wanted to go play a round at Heartwell one evening.

I was now about as tall as Dad, and we shared his clubs. It was a fun night, and I could match dad shot for shot. We would be to the right of the green and then to left and a par didn't seem posible for either one of us that night.

As it got late I teed off and hit a really nice drive. Dad hit his just in front of the green and as we approached the green I didn't see my ball and figured it had gone over the green. However, as I walked across the green there was my ball 3" from the hole. I pointed it out to Dad and then tapped it in for a birdie!

Several weeks later Dad and I made plans to play the par 3 course in Compton. The weather looked ominous, but we decided to go anyway.

It began to drizzle as we began our round. And again Dad and I shared his clubs.

It started raining pretty hard, and it appeared no one else was on the course. The next hole was along the fence of the ballfields of the school next door.

Dad teed off first and hit a nice drive, I was next and took a hard swing and the ball sailed down the fairway. I didn't follow my shot, I was looking at the ballfield off to the left.

Dad asked, "Why are you looking over there. Your ball went

straight down the fairway?"

"Well," I said, "my club went sailing over the fence."

The fence was an 8' chain-link fence, and Dad climbed over it and retrieved the club.

"Let's finish this hole and call it a day."

We walked back toward the clubhouse, we were both soaking wet by this time. Dad said, "Let's grab something to drink at the snack bar."

As we walked up to the window Dad ordered a V-8. I had never had a V-8, but wanting to be like Dad, I told the man that I would also like a V-8.

We were both handed these little cans and Dad took a long drink. I took a smaller drink and immediately spit it out.

"Tomato juice," I said. I hated tomato juice and tossed the rest in the trash!

I remember on the way back to the house enjoying the heat coming up from our heater in our '59 Ford Galaxy.

We laughed about my club sailing over the fence, and we laughed about my first can of V-8!

It was a very memorable day!

Chapter 25 -- A Bowl of Chili

Jerry lived halfway up the block when I was growing up. He was older, going to Poly when I was in 6th or 7th grade. Jerry had a 1962 Chevrolet Corvair. It was silver with a black interior, chrome rims, 4 speed and a chrome under-the-dash record player. At the time I thought this was a very cool car. Jerry would go out every Saturday morning that I remember and wash and wax his car, while playing 45's on the record player. I was usually on my front porch looking through my baseball cards as I watched Jerry tend to the Corvair. Occasionally I would walk up the street and sit and watch him work. Seems he usually had a Saturday night date and wanted the car to be perfect.

A year or so later I would go with my Dad to his body shop and help around the shop on Saturdays. Dad always had "loaner" cars for his customers to drive while he repaired and painted their cars. He would also buy wrecked cars from the salvage yards, repair the damage then keep them as "loaners" or flip them for some fast cash.

I was thinking about going with my Dad one Saturday, but I wasn't sure if this was a good week or not. Dad said he could use my help tearing down a pretty bad wreck that he had just gotten in, plus he told me he had bought a 1960 Corvair that he had just repainted.

I was now excited, thinking of the silver beauty that was always parked up the street.

After our regular stop at Winchell's Donuts, we arrived at the shop. When Dad opened the shop doors I quickly looked for the Corvair. "It's in the paint booth," Dad told me. I raced up to the walk-in door of the booth and opened it with great anticipation.

It looked nice and fresh, a shiny new paint job, but it was green. I didn't like this particular green and I was rather disappointed. I walked over to inspect the interior, it was a tri-color green and on the floor between the bucket seats there was no shifter. I quickly looked at the dash, and there just to the right of the steering wheel was a small black shift lever. It was an automatic. I had never heard of a Corvair that wasn't a manual shift.

At this point my enthusiasm for this Corvair was over. I walked back out of the booth, told Dad about my disappointment in the car and proceeded to follow him over to the wreck that he wanted me to work on.

As we walked up to the front of the Ford Econoline van, there was a lot of damage to the driver's side front end. As he usually did, Dad would rub his finger in the dust on the vehicle of where he wanted me to cut off the damaged body parts. As he showed me what to do with the driver's door, I noticed the window was half open, and the glass and the outside of the door had a lot of dried blood. I verified with Dad that this was indeed blood, and Dad told me the driver was killed in the accident. I removed the crushed bumper, got the air hose and the air chisel and was beginning to cut off the front body panels when Dad said he was going around the corner. "We'll go to lunch," he said, "when I get back." I removed most of the parts by noon, and Dad hadn't returned yet. I knew "around the corner" meant he was going for a drink at the 90/80 Club.

So while I waited I climbed into the cab of the Econoline. I turned on the radio, and as I did there on the floor was a black banana and a moldy bologna sandwich. This guy was killed while driving and eating his lunch I determined. I turned off the radio and climbed out of the van, it freaked me out being in a dead man's car!

Dad returned closer to 1:00 than noon, and he said, "Let's pull the Corvair out of the booth and we'll drive it to lunch." Dad said he had a spot down the street he wanted to try. It was an old white house on Lakewood Blvd. that a couple had converted to a small restaurant. Dad was told they made great chili. Dad and I both loved good chili. As we started off in the Corvair, it wasn't running right. The engine was missing and the car stalled several times, but we made it. The restaurant was less than a mile down the street.

As we entered, there were two small tables, one on each side of the door, and a lunch counter that had about eight stools. Dad said, "Let's eat at the counter."

We quickly decided to try the chili. Dad had a beer and I ordered a glass of milk. As the bowls of chili arrived, the waitress also places a bottle of Tabasco sauce in front of us. As we tasted the chili we both looked at each other thinking the same thing, this chili is HOT! Not hot from the stove, hot from the spices. We both kept eating, but before we left the restaurant our mouths still burning, we joked about the Tabasco, and wondered who could add that to the chili!

As we pulled away from the curb for the short drive back to the shop, the Corvair stalled. Dad re-started it and it stalled again. We were in the right traffic lane and several cars went around us.

I could now tell that Dad had been drinking, his actions were a little bit impaired. The car started again, Dad putting it in gear, it sounded like it again would stall. He tried to put it in neutral, but it ended up in reverse and lurched backwards. A car had stopped behind us and the Corvair hit the car behind us. My Dad and the other driver were discussing what had happened when the Sheriff arrived. I was certain that Dad would be in trouble because he had been drinking. After five minutes or so, the Sheriff came to talk with me. He said the other driver said my Dad was driving backwards and ran into him. The Sheriff asked me what had happened. I told him how the car kept stalling, wouldn't stay running! But driving in reverse? "No way I told him, the guy ran into us." I didn't know what else to say.

Dad then explained he owned the body shop just up the street and would take care of the small damage on the other driver's car. The other driver agreed and the Sheriff sent us on our way!

Just another day with an alcoholic father...

Chapter 26 -- Dad's Shop

During the summer of 1963, I'm excited about starting Hughes Junior High in the fall. I'm also getting excited about learning to drive! I'm having dreams about cars that drive by themselves by the time I reach sixteen, and I'm going to miss out on the real driving experience! So I ask my Dad if he'll teach me to drive. To my surprise he says, "Yes."

So one Saturday afternoon he takes me up to the Safeway parking lot and within minutes I'm behind the wheel of our new 1963 Ford station wagon driving around the parking lot like I've been doing it all my life! I was born to drive! After we've toured the lot numerous times, Dad says, "Ok, drive us home." So I pull out on 46th street, cross Atlantic and head to the house. I'm able to convince my Dad to let me drive around the neighborhood on several more afternoons before I need more of a challenge.

"Dad, I need to drive a stick shift." So, after constant reminders, my Dad says he'll bring home a car with stick shift this Saturday. Now my Dad owned his own body and fender business on the corner of Lakewood and Artesia. He had four or five "loaner" cars that customers could drive while their cars were in the shop for repairs.

Dad worked Monday thru Friday and half day on Saturdays. So this Saturday afternoon Dad drives home a 1952 Chevy coupe, beige in color with "three on the tree" as they say. So off we go back to the Safeway parking lot and my lesson with a stick shift. After stalling the car several times, I've got this mastered!

He teaches me to listen to the engine to know when to shift to second and then to third. I love this. It was more like really driving. Again, Dad lets me drive back to the house.

The following weekend I decided to go to work with my Dad for a half-day on Saturday, and I continued to do this for the rest of the summer. Dad tells me that he'll sell me the '52 Chevy for $32.00. I agree and will work a half-day on Saturdays for $2.00. Each Saturday I worked, I got $2.00 taken off what I owed for the car. This was great; I'm almost a 7th grader, and I have a job and a car!

Over the next year our Saturday routine was pretty slick: I leave the house about 7:00 a.m., hit the Winchell's at Del Amo and Paramount for my carton of milk, a maple bar and two crumb doughnuts. At work I would tear down wrecks, get lessons on bodywork; but the most fun was using the spray gun. At first all I shot was primer, but after I was showing a little bit of skill, I moved up to paint. At first I'd practice on torn-up car parts or on the wall, but eventually I shot a fender or two, and then my bicycle and surfboard.

One of my Dad's buddies was "Bob the chrome man." So he would come by every Saturday around 10:00, drop off a couple of bumpers that were finished and pick up whatever else my Dad had for him to re-chrome. Bob told me that if I took off all the interior window moldings of the '52, he'd chrome them for me! Wow, this was great! And then Bob and my Dad would tell me they were going around the corner and be back in a bit.

Well, I got my window frames chromed and reinstalled them

in my car. It looked really cool! Next were the rims and they turned out great as well! So I eventually got the car paid off and continued to work on Saturdays when it didn't interfere with school or sports.

The next summer between 7th and 8th grade I continued to go to the shop when I could. Bob continued to show up around 10:00, but they stopped returning by noon. Sometimes it was 1:00 or 2:00. A couple of times it was even later. I knew where they went, the 90/80 Club, a neighborhood bar on Artesia. My Dad had a deal with Los Altos Ford and did most of their bodywork on T-Birds. There were always several in the shop.

One Saturday being bored I was sitting in a new Thunderbird convertible with an 8-track tape player and several tapes in the glove box! The one I liked was "Hard Day's Night" by the Beatles. I played this all afternoon while waiting for Dad to return. To this day when I hear the opening chord for a "Hard Day's Night," I'm transported back to that Ford convertible, listening to the tape, and I can almost smell the many great smells of paint and body filler that permeated the shop!

I had been working on the '52 Chevy and was getting close to painting it. On the way to the shop one morning my Dad says, "Your car is gone!"

Gone, what does that mean? "I let your Uncle Ed drive it the other day, and he didn't bring it back! Your Grandmother said he took off to Oklahoma to get work with your Uncle Ben!" I never saw my 1952 Chevy coupe again!

I didn't go to work with my Dad for a while after that. But one Friday evening he asked me to go to work with him in the morning. He had something to show me. I agreed, and in the morning we still went to Winchell's for our same breakfast. When we got to the shop, we got the doors opened, the lights on, and Dad says, "Let's go out back." Out behind the shop was a 1948 Ford panel truck, and Dad asks me what do I think?

"Why, I think it's pretty cool," I said.

Dad says, "I just bought it for $50.00, and if you want it, you can have it to take the place of the Chevy!"

"Done," I told him. So once again I had a project to work on. So it's back to the shop when I didn't have sports. I got it cleaned up, the little dents taken care of and planned on painting it "competition orange."

Saturdays, though, are getting to really be a drag. Dad gives me money for lunch and then goes off to the 90/80 Club. I'm usually lucky if I see him by 3:00 or 4:00 p.m.

There's a coffee shop across the street on Artesia that has a pretty good burger and fries, and I always add a salad with Thousand Island dressing. So, one Saturday after lunch, I sat in this 1963 Chevy Corvette pretending to drive it down the drag strip, quickly banging through the gears.

But this only entertains me for so long, and I decide to actually take it out for a spin! I start it up and back out of the shop, turn into the first neighborhood street I can turn on and spend the next 15 minutes cruising the streets. I decided I better get back so as not to get caught, and I drove back to the shop, pull it in and turn it off!

I'm thinking that was really fun. I didn't get caught, and I doubt that Dad will be back anytime soon. So off I go again, and this car is really fun to drive! When I bring it back this time, I speed into the shop, hit the brakes and tap the car parked in front of it!

I jumped out and check for damage, but there is none. So when I go to work from this point on, the first thing I look for is which car can I get out easily to take for a joy ride. There were plenty but none as cool as that Vette.

As 9th grade starts I'm really busy on Saturdays with sports, girls and hanging out! Not much time for the shop. One

Saturday between football and basketball seasons I went to work with my Dad to see if we can spray the panel truck. It doesn't fit in the spray booth, so we plastic off all the cars in the shop so we can spray it in one of the bays. Dad tells me to "mask it off" and "tack it down," and he'll be right back. Several hours later he's back and we are mixing paint. He starts painting one of the big side panels, which is contrary to what he's taught me so far. Half the side is painted and the color is a really cool orange, but it is starting to "run" all the way down the side! Dad stops painting and tells me to get rags and paint thinner and to start wiping off the paint.

Dad puts down the gun and helps me, but I can really smell alcohol, and I think he's pretty wasted. Well, Dad heads off and tells me to unmask it and put it back outside, saying, "We'll paint it next week!"

That afternoon turned out to be my last Saturday at the shop and the last time I saw the panel truck! By 5:00 p.m. my Dad hadn't come back yet, so I called the 90/80 club and was told they didn't know Chuck Mosley!

I called the house, and no one answered! Well, I sat there until well after dark and decided to lock up the shop and drive the panel truck home. As I head out I'm pissed off and afraid that a cop might stop me, so I decide to go to my Grandma's house, as it was closer.

That turned out to be a big mistake because now my grandparents are involved, and they're really mad! My Grandma drove me home and got into it with my Mom. Things were never the same! For the next several months all Mom and Dad did was fight.

Occasionally they'd go out to dinner, just the two of them. Whenever that happened, I would jump into whatever car my Dad had driven home and go out and cruise the Country Club or Wrigley districts with a buddy or two! I was getting really good at power sliding around corners and driving like a crazy man! Never got caught, never had an accident and never was stopped by a cop!

One day I got home from school, and my Mom informed me that we are moving to her mom's house, over off of Del Amo on Silva St. Well, this really sucks. I didn't want to leave the house or stay with this Grandma!

Her house was so boring! I had a twin bed off of her kitchen and would stay out as late as I could with my girlfriend and her family so I wouldn't have to be at Grandma's house. I remember that I'd get up really early, turn on the radio, I remember "Lightening Strikes" and "I'm So Lonesome I Could Cry" were the songs being played, as well as Sonny and Cher. I would leave for school before anyone else was up, walk to my house where sometimes I'd see my Dad, change my clothes and head to Hughes.

Often, if I was early I'd stop at Fiddlers Three, sit at the counter and get a stack of pancakes and a glass of milk. One day when I got home from school, Mom was really pissed at me. "What did I do?" I asked.

"Spoke with your Dad today, and he said you ditched school with your girlfriend and was at the house with her when he came home early!" Well, that didn't happen, and it took a lot to convince her that it wasn't true. Several days later we moved back to the house, and Dad had moved to an apartment on Atlantic, north of Del Amo. Mom had decided that my Dad was hallucinating!

One Saturday afternoon/early evening I decided to walk up Atlantic and find out where he was staying! I saw his car and figured which apartment he was in. I visited for just a short while and couldn't believe how bad he looked, and this place was a smelly dump!

I told my Mom about my visit, and she called my

grandmother, Dad's mom, who went and picked him up and took him to her house. The following week Grandma said he was going into the hospital and was going to get help! That Thursday Mom decided to take my brother, sister and me to Mexico City Restaurant for dinner. It was always one of our favorites! After a good dinner we headed home. As we drove into the driveway our next-door neighbor came out and asked to speak with my Mom. We went into the house and waited. As she came in I could see something was wrong. "What is it?" we asked.

"Your Father died in the hospital today!" Well, my brother Chris burst into tears and ran off to his bedroom, and Mom followed after. I sat there for a moment and then headed out the door. I couldn't believe it, as I walked up to the Bixby Knolls Shopping Center. I walked to Thrifty's, in through the back doors, to the phone booths. I called my girlfriend and asked if she could meet me.

"My Dad just died!" I sat at the park and cried well into the night. She and her family were great support for me during this time. I will always be thankful for that!

The next few days were kind of a blur. I remember sitting by myself one day after gym class, and Coach Zielinski came out of his office just to say hey!

"I won't be at baseball practice tomorrow; I've got to go to my Dad's funeral."

"What?" He said.

"My Dad died Thursday and his funeral is tomorrow."

At his funeral I was very surprised to see a number of my Hughes classmates there. I cried when I walked past my Dad's coffin and, touching his hand, it didn't feel real. I cried once more after that day. It was on an evening in 1992, the day after my brother died. That's it, three times in 50 years.

Little did I know that this was only the beginning of several years of turmoil in my life. A few days after Dad's funeral was the father/son sports banquet at Hughes. I wanted to go because I was getting the Outstanding Baseball player award for the second straight year, but I thought I'd stand out being there alone. Mom convinced me to go, so I showered, dressed and walked to school. When I arrived, most were standing outside talking before we were allowed to enter and find seats.

This was going to be awkward, I thought, and looked for a place to wander off. Suddenly Mr. Burden walked up to me, placed his arm on my shoulder and said, "Chuck, tonight you're with us!" I'll never forget that act of kindness by Greg and his father, and I did win the award that night!

Well, Dad left us broke, and Mom had to go to work. We went to the body shop and loaded up all the tools he had left and also the huge air compressor in the back. Mom was trying to sell off the compressor and some of his body tools. One morning I saw a car with a trailer pull up in front of the house. "A buyer," I said to myself. I went to my room to put on a t-shirt as the doorbell rang.

I opened the door, and standing there was Uncle Ed, the guy that stole my Chevy! "What do you want?" I asked.

"I came by to pick up your Dad's tools. He would've wanted me to have them."

"Get the fuck out of here!" I told him and slammed the door.

I tried to adjust to the fact that Dad was gone, but I kept having dreams that I'd awaken some day, and he'd be there. It was hard for the reality to set in.

My Mom sold our Ford station wagon and got a job. She bought a '59 Volvo (It sure wasn't fancy) to replace the station wagon. After several months, Mom started going out. Her favorite place was Lucy's in North Long Beach. I kept myself busy that summer and was looking forward to starting at Long Beach Poly.

As school approached my Mom was dating a guy named Ralph. One Sunday morning I walked in to my Mom's bedroom, and she was there asleep with someone that I didn't know. I quickly got dressed and left for the day. That evening when I came home my Mom told me she was with Ralph, and they were going to get married.

This seemed awfully soon, and my brother and I didn't like the idea. As he started to come around he seemed like an OK guy, but my brother didn't seem to like him. He and Mom had some strange ideas. He was going to be the head of the family, and we were expected to be fine with that.

Well, I had my girlfriend's family I could be with so I stayed away as much as possible. It seems like they married in the fall. Then he brought home his two daughters for us to meet and announced that they would be moving in with us.

Suddenly, we had three new people living in our house, and a new head of household. As soon as they were married Mom quit her job and went back to being a mom. Ralph's girls were the same age as Chris and me. My bedroom was split, and I ended up with a 6x10 bedroom with a bath I shared with my brother. It had a quick access to the front door. This now made it possible to come and go undetected which was great.

As I started Poly in the fall I was asked to try out for the three top fraternities at school. This was really great, and I decided to try out for Comus. The first six weeks were a breeze as I played sports with some of the guys, and they made sure I was protected.

Ralph and Mom had planned a family outing to the Los Angeles History Museum with all of us. I didn't really wish to go, but I was free that Saturday and said I would go. As we were walking out the door the phone rang, and it was a Comus guy asking me where I was. He told me that I was supposed to be at his house. I told him that I knew nothing about it and now

I had plans. He said that Jeff was supposed to tell me and to get over there as quick as I could. Mom and Ralph said I had to go with them, so I told this guy that I just couldn't come and hung up.

That Tuesday night this asshole took a board and beat the crap out of the backside of my thighs! I stayed there and took it. But walking home that night I decided no one would ever do that to me again. And no one has ever physically hurt me since.

The next day at school I told the Comus guys I was done. Several of them tried to get me to change my mind that week, but I had made up my mind. So basically that was the end of my Poly social life.

Most of the kids I hung out with at Hughes were in clubs as well as the guys I played baseball with. To this day the guys and gals tell you that nothing is different if you're not in a club! But to the kids on the outside you are so excluded from most social activities.

So in the span of about six months my father died, Mom had to declare bankruptcy, I had a step family living with us and high school didn't start off very well at all!

Chapter 27 -- Parliamentarian

At Hughes in 9th grade I chose to take Student Government. This was an elective class and met during first period at 7:00 a.m. Our teacher was Mrs. Burtle, the Girls Vice Principal. During the first semester I was elected Parliamentarian. I had to learn Parliamentary Procedure and oversee our Student Council meetings. I enjoyed the class, although I wasn't a fan of Mrs. Burtle or having a class at 7:00 in the morning. But I had a lot of friends in the class.

As the second semester started, I had completed my duties as Parliamentarian and was starting to enjoy the coming of spring. One morning, sitting in class as the bell rang, Mrs. Burtle came into class, a little out of breath and announced that she had an appointment and had to leave. Great news, I thought. We can go outside and wait for everyone else to arrive for school! So I was a little surprised as she said we had to go to the library for the remainder of class.

As we got up from our desks, Mrs. Burtle rushed out of the classroom and headed to her car. As we walked out of the classroom, room 202, and walked up the hall toward the library, I was thinking how hungry I was and how boring the library would be. As we walked past the office and out of the 200 building into the breezeway I asked Betsy, who was walking with me, "Hey Bets, let's go to breakfast!"

She looked at me and quickly replied, "Sure, let's go." So Betsy and I made a left turn and walked out of the school and headed down Roosevelt to Park Pantry. Looking around, no one seemed to notice that we'd left the group. We walked down the hill to Park Pantry, were seated in a booth and ate breakfast as we chatted.

Afterwards, we walked back just in time to get to our homeroom classes. As the day went on, I figured we were in the clear.

When 7th period came, a girl walked into my classroom and handed the teacher a call slip. "Chuck, you need to go to the office," the teacher said. Wow, busted I thought. What else could it be? As I took the call slip from the teacher and walked out in the hall, I read, "Go to Mrs. Burtle's office."

When I walked in, the secretary sent me right in. Well, it turned out that as Mrs. Burtle left school she drove down Roosevelt Drive towards Atlantic and saw Betsy and me headed down the street. She asked why, and did I think she wouldn't find out? So I told her that I was hungry, felt that the library would be boring and that we were just going there for busy work. She also brought up the fact that I had had my Friday Niters card suspended recently! "This is not what we expect from our student government students," she said.

Well, Betsy and I were suspended for three days and were kicked out of Student Government class. My Friday Niters card was taken for the remainder of the school year. When I got home that afternoon and explained what had happened to my Mom, she was a bit disappointed in me, however, not really mad. So actually, this turned out pretty darn good, no more 7 o'clock class, three days off from school, and I didn't really like going to Friday Niters!

Plus, I had a really nice breakfast with my friend Betsy.

Go Hughes '66!!

Chapter 28 -- King Fish

During the summer of 1966, life was a series of ups and downs; the recent death of my Father, my Mom dating and remarrying, two step-sisters moving into the house and getting ready to start high school. Plus, I had just started playing Connie Mack baseball for John Herbold. My girlfriend and her family seemed to be my only sanctuary at the time.

In August one of my friends, Bill, invited me to spend a week in the Sierra's at Virginia Lakes, up above Mammoth just outside of Lee Vining, California. I quickly accepted the invitation to go. Bill and I were going with Bill's father, Dr. Penn, his older brother Tom and his friend Bruce. I was dropped off at their house near Hughes Junior High School and met the family as we packed up their station wagon for what turned out to be a long day of driving.

It took forever to get things packed up and to get on the road. Bill's father was not a very fast driver, and it felt like forever just to get out of Los Angeles. After several hours on the road, we stopped for gas and a snack. Bill's older brother Tom now took the wheel.

Tom attempted to make up some time, but Dr. Penn monitored his speed and constantly told him to slow down. I'm not sure how long it took to get to Bishop, but when we pulled into the Safeway parking lot, I couldn't wait to get out of the car. Into Safeway we went as Dr. Penn pushed the shopping cart up and down the aisles with Bill and Tom helping their dad pick out the groceries that we would need for the next week.

Bruce and I trailed along behind, and I got to know Bruce a bit. He was a great guy as it turned out and was in Comus with Tom at Poly.

After we loaded the groceries into the back of the station wagon, it was time to complete our journey to the lake. I was hoping it would be less than an hour, but it turned out it was closer to two. It was an hour to Lee Vining and then almost another hour up the dirt road to the lakes and our cabin.

We unpacked, and Bill and I walked to lake as Tom and his dad started dinner. Not sure what we ate for dinners that week, but I know we had a lot of cereal and plenty of sandwiches during the day. The four guys decided to keep track of the trout that we got, and the one who caught the most would be crowned "King Fish."

After the first day or two, the two older boys did their own thing, and Bill and I did the same. We fished, hiked and did a lot of talking about Hughes, Poly, sports and our girlfriends, who were best friends at the time. It was great to be away from the turmoil of everyday life.

On the morning we were going to pack up and head home, I was second in the fish count, and we had only a few hours left to fish. I picked a spot on the lake that we hadn't tried, cast in my line and caught a fish within minutes. Baiting my hook again, I sent my line out into the same spot and boom, another fish. I pulled in a total of five from that spot, carried them back to the cabin and was given the title "King Fish." I have that written on my old tackle box still today.

Not long after we returned home, school started. What a culture shock. On the first day of school about fourth period, I got a call slip to go to the office. I had no idea why.

As I walked into the office I was told to step into the office to the left. Sitting there was Coach Matz, whom I recognized but had never met.

"Mosley!" he said. "Where the hell have you been?"

I didn't have a clue what he was talking about.

"We started practicing two weeks ago, why weren't you out there with us?" I explained that I didn't know anything about it. He couldn't believe I was unaware that practice had already started.

"I'm rearranging your schedule, be there tomorrow with your cleats."

The next afternoon I walked into the locker room, was introduced to the JV coach who handed me off to the equipment manager. Not much to choose from: my helmet was too tight, pants too loose and my pads wanted to slip as I walked.

Out on the field, two guys from Hughes were taking snaps at quarterback who weren't able to make our Hughes team.

"Go over and work with the linemen," I was told.

"Wow, this really sucks," I thought. I'm not a lineman, and those two aren't quarterbacks.

Back at home, I was invited to join three different "fraternities." At school it was apparent that this could be a difficult decision as my friends from Hughes were split between these fraternities, Chaparral, Comus and Sphinx. Plus, the guys that invited me to join were all friends as well.

I finally made my choice: Comus! Tom and Bruce from the fishing trip were in Comus, and Bill was going out for Comus as well, so that's whom I choose.

As all this was going on: my father died four months earlier, my Mom re-married, a strange family moved into my house, my brother's behavior became rebellious, I became a nobody in a sport I loved, I started high school and pledged a fraternity. My skin broke out in cysts, mainly on my back and shoulders, but also on my face and neck. I became very self- conscious, more withdrawn and worried that I'd lose my girlfriend, the only constant in my life.

I quit football, too much pain. I'd wear a t-shirt under my pads, and it would be covered in blood by the time I got home from practice each night.

I quit Comus one night after a guy beat the crap out of my thighs because he was pissed at me.

Swimming and going to the beach became too embarrassing, because I couldn't take my shirt off. A doctor tried to treat the condition with very little success. It finally cleared up about the time we graduated high school in 1969. But the scars, both physically and emotionally have stayed.

A doctor later told me it was most likely caused from all the stress at the time and that I didn't have any other release...

Chapter 29 -- Moon River

We just arrived back at Hughes. It was Saturday and the Hughes 9th grade basketball team had just won our 4th game in a row. After showering and leaving the locker room, several of us stood outside wondering what to do the rest of the day. Greg suggested we walk to his house and play some more basketball. I agreed, as did Mike Burley and Mike Lane.

As we left Hughes we decided to stop at the Taco Bell down the street first, and then off to Greg's house on Country Club Drive.

Arriving at Greg's the four of us headed upstairs to Greg's room so he could change. Thirty minutes or so went by and we slowly headed downstairs to get on with our basketball game.

Walking through the house we could hear Greg's Mom playing the piano in a room just off their living room. Greg headed to where she was playing so we could all say "Hi".

Greg's Mom reminded me of June Clever, always dressed nicely, ready for a luncheon or a Lady's tea.

As we walked into the room she stopped playing the piano and greeted us warmly. As we talked Greg's Dad came in from the kitchen and joined the conversation. As we started to head outdoors, Greg's Mom started playing Moon River on the piano.

"Hey," Greg's Dad said, "You boys know Moon River?" Sure, we all said as he suggested we sing it as Mrs. Burden played the piano. Being shy, I was not really into this, but I figured I could manage to sing along with the other three guys.

We must have sung Moon River at least three times. As we finished the third time, I thought we actually sounded pretty good. Well, so did Mr. Burden. He applauded, as did Greg's Mom. I should get you guys into a recording studio!

As we made our way out to the driveway and began our two on two-basketball game I began thinking, they're so rich, I wouldn't be surprised if we were in a studio soon! As the game went on, I would rebound and pass the ball out to Mike B, my teammate, as he and I were up on the other two.

The game became more competitive as those kinds of games usually did. After one errant shot we all jumped for a rebound. As the ball bounced off our fingertips Mike B. let out a yell of pain and bent over holding his left hand. As I looked closely, I could see blood coming out between his fingers and dripping on the driveway. Mike had caught his ring on the rain gutter that ran along the Burden's garage. Greg and I moved Mike's hand away so we could see if it was bad. His ring was no longer round and the skin on his finger was hanging loose, it was torn all the way to the bone,

Greg ran to the house and quickly retrieved his Dad. Greg's Dad was able to remove the ring and proceeded to wrap a dishtowel around Mike's bloody hand.

As the garage door opened, I noticed that they had two beautiful Lincoln Continentals parked side by side.

Greg, his Dad and Mike climbed into one of the Continentals and headed off to the emergency room.

The other Mike and I watched them drive away as he and I slowly started our walk back to our houses.

On Monday Mike B. was fine, a big bandage covering his ring finger as he relayed the details of what had happened, as the other students gathered around.

Moon River? Nope, we never sang again!

Chapter 30 -- Summer 1966

I played baseball at Poly for three years, 1967-68-69. In the summer of 1966 Coach Herbold plucked a group of 9th graders from Hughes, Washington and Franklin to play Connie Mack and American Legion ball. We played in three or four different leagues. I think we played about 75 games that summer.

We didn't win many that summer, but that wasn't the point. We were to get ready for the Moore League season of 1968! So we went out game after game, and we were only l4 or 15 years old, playing against players that were juniors and seniors, and occasionally players that had already graduated from high school!

So, like I said, we didn't win much that first season, but we learned a lot about how to play baseball the right way: Herbold's way!

The first game I was invited to was with the Long Beach Blues team, and the game was at Blair Field. Now this was a far cry from playing at Cherry Park or Silverado Park. It was a real ballpark with dugouts, pitching mound and bullpens. I was really nervous that day because I only knew the other four players from Hughes.

The game went by quickly, and in about the sixth inning

Coach Herbold told me to "go and warm up." So off to the bullpen I went to start throwing.

So I threw 10 or 12 pitches, and this guy walked up to me and asked me if I'm warm. "Yes," I told him. "My name is Randy. I pitched for Poly this year, and I just graduated."

"Randy Moffitt?" I ask.

"Yes," he replied. "Let's see your curve ball. Not my best pitch, but I throw a couple. Do you throw a slider?" he asked.

"No," I answered.

"Well, you throw a lot like I do, so you need to throw a slider! I'll be at your next game, and we can work on it before the game."

"Thanks," I said as I heard Herbold yell, "Mosley, get out there!"

So I ran out to the mound at Blair, and I was thinking that this was so cool! I started warming up, and I immediately realized that throwing off a mound like that felt like I was throwing down hill. I liked it!

My fastball seemed even harder when throwing off a mound. So I pitched the last inning of the game. They didn't score, and I was so nervous I only threw fastballs.

After the game, Herbold told me I looked good out there. Wow, that was pretty fun!

And Randy, the sister of tennis star Billie Jean King, went on to pitch for 12 seasons for the San Francisco Giants.

Chapter 31 – American Legion

There are hundreds of unwritten rules in baseball. I learned a lot of them playing for John Herbold:

"You don't play baseball, you work it!"

"No one can throw a fastball past Mays, except Koufax and God!"

"A walk's a run!"

"Practice doesn't make perfect; perfect practice makes perfect!"

"Never walk the lead-off batter!"

Well, Herbold had lots of these sayings. He also liked to needle players. I pitched an American Legion game in '66 at Leuzinger High School. In right field just beyond the chain link fence was a tin maintenance building. In the first inning, their third batter in the line-up, a tall left-hander, drilled a home run over the right field fence and landed on the tin building. It made a very specific sound as it hit this building.

The next time I faced him, in the third or fourth inning, "Crack!" he drilled another shot off me and again hit the building.

As I stated before, we were mostly ninth graders playing against high school juniors and seniors. Well, I pitched the entire game and we lost 7-0. The left-handed batter hit a third home run off me before the game was over, knocking in all runs!

So this became Herbold's "needle" for me for the next couple of years. To motivate me he'd yell, "Mosley, I can still hear the ball landing on that tin building!" This usually pissed me off, and I usually would bear down and throw harder, giving Herbold the desired result.

On July 4th, 1967, we were playing another Legion game, this time on a Sunday, and we were playing at Wilson High School. I was pitching a really good game, a 1-0 shutout through eight innings -- and they hadn't gotten a hit!

I took the mound for the ninth inning. I walked the first batter -- a cardinal sin for a pitcher.

Well, Herbold called time and headed toward me on the mound! I could tell he was pissed as he made his way towards the mound.

He was shouting, "A walk's a run!"

"Mosley, you never walk the lead-off hitter! "Give me the ball."

So I walked to the dugout, pissed at myself, and also pissed at Herbold. I was usually pissed at Herbold when I pitched. It was just the relationship we had.

Well, my relief pitcher gave up two hits and we lost 2-1! Coach Powell came over and told me, "That's tough, you know you had a no-hitter."

"Yeah, I knew," and so did Herbold; but, a lesson was learned. Never walk a lead-off hitter, and a walk's a run!

Chapter 32 -- Dooley's Hardware Store

One of my grandmothers worked at Dooley's for 15 years, at least! She was a cashier at the south entrance of the main building. When I needed some extra money, I would go to her house on Silva and mow and edge her lawn.

On this particular occasion she happened to mention that they were hiring part-time workers for Christmas. Having a girlfriend and needing money for a car, plus I was turning 16 in April, I walked to Dooley's and put in an application.

A couple of days later I was called in for an interview and was hired on the spot. I would work in the "housewares" department and would be paid $1.50 an hour. This was minimum wage in 1966.

The job was really easy: move boxes from the loading docks to the storage area upstairs and then bring down whatever the manager wanted or needed to stock the shelves. Sometimes there wasn't much to do for an hour or two, so I came up with a way to have some fun and make the time go by quicker.

The storage area in the attic had a series of tracks that you would place the boxes on and then roll them along to their proper area for storage. I could take a box of toasters or mixers, maybe a dozen in the box, and get a running start, jump on the box and ride it to the end of the rollers. This turned out to be fun, and it would make my day go by much faster.

One of the benefits of working Sundays was a free lunch in the employee lunchroom. There were various things to eat, sandwiches, cans of soup or beans, but my favorite was to make a hamburger on the stove, add mayo, mustard, relish, and for cheese they had a can of Cheez Whiz. I had never had this before, but it tasted really good!

Usually I would make a second. Well, the job only lasted three weeks, but I made enough to complete all my Christmas shopping.

When school was out in June, I went back to Dooley's and applied for a summer job. I was hired on the spot and this time would be working in the TV department.

Mainly the job was the same, stock the TVs in the storage area and then, when a salesman sold one, bring it out and load it into the customer's vehicle. This time I would be making a $1.65!

The first Sunday I had to work I went over to the lunchroom, and sitting on the sink next to the mustard and ketchup was a can of Cheez Whiz! Life was good.

Some days there would be two of us scheduled to work. This was fun because I had someone to talk with, and we would alternate bringing out the televisions, but we had nothing to do a lot of the time.

My co-worker was about 20, and he had a tattoo on his forearm of a naked female. He was not proud of the "gal" and often wished it wasn't there. So one slow afternoon he asked me if I would help him remove it.

"Sure," I said. "How are we going to do it?" He told me to cover for him, and he'd be right back.

When he came back, he carried a brown paper sack. As he removed the items, needles, cotton balls, alcohol, gauze, bleach and peroxide, he told me he wanted me to poke the tattoo with needles, and we would pour bleach and peroxide into the "holes" and see if we could bleach it out. Sounded like a great plan to me.

So I started poking him with a needle all along the outline of the girl. He winced in pain now and then, but insisted I continue. After a couple of hours of this, it appeared it might work, but he had little drops of blood all over his arm.

Finally, as the day ended, we poured bleach, peroxide and alcohol on his arm and then wrapped it in gauze. My co-worker didn't show up for several days, and I heard that he had some kind of infection.

As my summer was coming to an end, I was told they were looking to hire two workers at the new Wayne's Richfield on the corner of Atlantic and San Antonio Drive. The station would be completed about the time school would start in September. It was time to transition!

Chapter 33 -- Night Fog

As I began my long walk home, about a mile or a mile and a quarter, it was very still. I always liked my walk home when the fog had rolled in. Leaving my girlfriend's house near Cherry Park, the smells were alive! I could hear the power lines buzzing, and the theme from "Get Smart" was playing in my head. The television had been on while we "hung out" together.

I always walked down San Antonio Dr., across Orange, through Bixby Knolls Park, and then across the parking lot behind the shopping center. It was then a short walk after crossing Atlantic, along 45th Street, and then down the hill of my block on Pasadena.

I had a curfew in ninth grade. It started out at 11:00 p.m., but I had talked my Mom into letting me leave my girlfriend's house at 11:00 and being home by 11:30. As I walked down the hill to my house, everything seemed normal. I walked into the house and the television was on. Mom was sitting on the couch watching an old movie.

I quickly wondered if I was late. I was never sure, I never wore a watch. I thought back to a minute ago, was Dad home?

Yeah, one of his two '56 Buick loan cars was parked at the curb.

"Hey, Mom, what's going on?"

"Your Dad came home late, and I couldn't sleep. Thought I'd sit up and watch television."

She asked how my evening was, and I answered, "Good." We just "hung out" and watched TV.

"It's really foggy out," I said.

"When I was a young girl, I loved being out in the fog," she said. "During the war we had to have 'black-out shades' so enemy planes couldn't see anything if they attacked us at night. My friends and I would wander around the neighborhood, and you could sneak up to a window and "flick" the blinds, and they would suddenly roll-up, scaring the people inside. It was better than ringing doorbells," she said. "We'd also climb up and hang out on the railroad tracks that crossed above Atlantic just north of Del Amo."

I asked Mom what she was watching, and she replied, "Just an old movie with Van Johnson." She explained that Van Johnson became a heartthrob during the war because he was one of the actors that stayed in Hollywood and didn't go off to fight.

As we watched the end of the movie, Mom continued talking until the test pattern came on the TV. Since neither of us seemed to be tired, Mom turned on the radio that hung on the wall. It looked like an old telephone. She dialed it to a radio show, something called "Night Owls." It was a kind of talk radio, and the calls that night seemed to mainly be about UFOs.

As it got later, Mom kept talking about her childhood and then began discussing the strange, but interesting phone calls that were now coming on the radio.

I was rather fascinated by the calls, but I was really enjoying hearing about my Mom's childhood in North Long Beach. It seemed like so long ago, but Mom was only 17 years old when I was born, so it really wasn't that long ago.

After several hours had passed, Mom showed no signs of

slowing down. I remember learning a lot about Mom that night.

Several weeks later, I was home, and Mom needed to go to the laundromat. The washer was broken, and the repair guy hadn't showed up. Dad had gotten home later than usual and had gone to bed. My brother was staying at a friend's house, and my sister Kelly was in bed.

I told Mom I would go with her, hoping to hear more stories of her youth. It was another foggy night.

I also grabbed my sister's small portable record player and an album by "Little Anthony and the Imperials." I wasn't sure where this album came from or who left it at the house, but thought I'd give it a listen.

As we pulled up to the laundromat behind Vons, only one lady was inside, and she was folding her clothes. When she left, I went out to the car and brought in the record player. In front of the window was a Formica folding table with an outlet behind it. I plugged in the record player and put on the album.

It took several hours for Mom to do the laundry. It was close to 2:00 a.m. when we finished. I heard more stories about Mom and Dad attending Lindberg and Jordan, about some of their friends who still lived in Long Beach, and how her Mother had divorced three times and the effects it had on her childhood.

I must have played that album several times all the way through, and then just played, "Going Out Of My Head," "Hurt so Bad" and "Tears on my Pillow" maybe another five or six times.

The songs later seemed so apropos when my Father passed away a month or so later.

Chapter 34 -- My '56 Chevy

Back in 1967, I could not wait to get my drivers license. My Grandmother "Birdie" had a 1956 Chevy that she had purchased brand new, and it had only 56,000 miles on the odometer.

She worked at Dooley's Hardware store as a cashier and several months before my 16th birthday, her car was stolen from the Dooley's parking lot. Grandma went out and purchased a new 1967 Chevy Impala and then several weeks later her '56 Chevy was discovered abandoned and stripped in an alley in Compton. Her insurance company totaled the car and valued what was left at $100.00.

Grandma called me and said if I wanted the car, she would have it towed to my house and I could pay the $100.00. I was so excited and couldn't wait for it to arrive.

When it was finally dropped off at the house, I went and inspected my "new" car. The exterior was all there except the bumpers; the interior was missing door panels, sun visors and the radio. The worst part was under the hood. The carburetor, intake manifold, exhaust manifolds and heads were all missing. I didn't have any experience with engine mechanics. My Dad had taught me some bodywork and how to prep and paint a car before he died 10 months earlier.

My new friend Bob was taking auto shop at Poly and assured

me that this was not very major. So it was off to the junkyards in Wilmington to start pricing and purchasing parts. I soon knew what everything would cost and I started buying parts whenever I got paid.

When my sixteenth birthday arrived, the car was not yet together. I was still lacking some parts. But after school on April 26, 1967, my 16th birthday, Mom and I drove to the DMV on Willow so I could take my drivers test.

Mom's car was a 1959 Volvo that she had purchased after selling the family station wagon to save money when Dad died. The Volvo was a faded red color and the accelerator stuck when you stopped at a light and engaged the clutch. So as I came to a stop I had to push in the clutch with one foot and with the other put it under the gas pedal and pull it back to get the car to idle at a normal rate.

As the instructor climbed into the Volvo with his clipboard, I was concerned about the car idling too fast and him thinking there was a problem with the car and maybe cancelling my test. As we went through the driving test, I worked really hard to keep the idle under control. As we pulled back into the parking lot, the examiner said to me, "You seemed a little pre-occupied." As I walked back into the DMV, I'm thinking he's not going to pass me because I was trying to keep the car idling normal.

I walked up to his window expecting bad news, but he smiled and said, "You passed with a score of 95. If you had been a little more focused on the test, I'd have given you 100%." Well, I didn't really care, I had my drivers license in my hand. The greatest event in my life up to this point! I had been waiting for this day since I was in 6th grade.

After we got back to the house Mom told me I could take the car and I was off! It was probably a month later that Bob and I fired up the '56 Chevy in my backyard.

That car went through various transformations during my school years. We cruised in it. I dated in it, listened to a lot of great music with my Muntz 4-track tape player and eventually raced it at Lions Drag Strip.

But it taught me to set goals, budget money and how to mechanically re-build an entire car! Best $100.00 I ever spent.

My '56 Chevy

Chapter 35 -- Step Father

When my Father died in June of '66, my Mom had to get a job. Being left a mortgage to pay and three kids to raise, she had little choice. She didn't like working, and often came home telling me about her lousy day. Several months after starting work, my Mom started going to Lucy's in North Long Beach for "dinner" on Friday and Saturday nights.

Later that summer, Mom introduced us to Ralph. Ralph was an electrician, divorced and had three daughters. By the time school started, they were married.

My bedroom was walled off, and I ended up with a small six feet wide room, and two of Ralph's daughters moved into what used to be my room.

Ralph and my Mom had strange ideas on how this would work. Ralph was now going to be the "Captain," and the one in charge. That didn't sit well with me or my brother Chris. Mom got what she was looking for, someone to help her raise the kids, and she was able to quit work and go back to being a housewife. The two "step-sisters" were OK. One was my age and the other two years younger. The one my age went to Wilson, and the younger sister was in junior high, near Wilson.

This is when I began to work, because I needed my own money. Dooley's was my job that summer and then on to

Wayne's Richfield.

Life was really strange now. My brother Chris began to rebel and began getting into trouble. I just tried to stay away.

My Mom and Ralph thought it would be good to take a weekend trip together so we could get to know each other better. Family time!

Ralph had friends that had a nice boat at Lake Mead. At the last minute our two step sisters got out of going, and it was now my brother and sister, Mom and Ralph. The excitement level was very low.

We climbed into Ralph's 1960 Ford, two-door station wagon and headed out of town one Friday night. Bored and miserable was the feeling Chris and I had.

About 11:00 p.m. we were about 20 minutes outside of Baker, and the generator light came on in the Ford wagon. As the headlights started to dim considerably, we could see the gas station sign up ahead.

After pulling into the station, we all headed to the restrooms as Ralph spoke to the attendant. When I returned to the car, Ralph informed us that they may have a set of brushes for the generator that might work. We had to push the car into the service bay, as the battery was now dead.

They closed the bay door, and Ralph and the attendant proceeded to pull the generator out of the car. Mom, Chris and my little sister sat in the car while I moved around the service bay trying to keep from going crazy.

Looking out the service bay door, I saw an old Oldsmobile pull into the station. It was a '55 or '56. It drove past the island and around the corner of the station, ringing the bell as it pulled through.

The attendant, seeing me by the door, asked if he needed to go out. "No," I said. "It didn't stop for gas."

I walked up to check the progress on the repairs and then

went back to roving around the service bay. I was at the rear of the station wagon, my back to the office door, when I heard what sounded like someone approaching, sloshing in water. It sounded like someone that had water in their shoes.

I turned around, and there was a man standing there. As I looked at him, he had blood running down his shirt and pants, and it was collecting in his shoes. I looked up at the man's face and saw that his neck had been sliced open, almost from ear to ear. The gash in his neck was at least two inches wide, and the blood was flowing.

"Ralph," I hollered! Ralph and the attendant looked up, saw the man and came rushing over. They walked him into the office, sat him down and called for help. They got him off in an ambulance, and I was left to give a statement on what I saw.

I described the car, what direction it came from and where I saw it stop. It seemed like hours that we were in that station. The generator was fixed and with a jump-start we were back on the highway.

The next morning we went to the lake and met Ralph's friends. They turned out to be nice, seemed very old, and they were both alcoholics. Just how I wanted to spend my weekend!

Chapter 36 -- Wayne's Richfield

In the fall of 1967 they were just finishing the construction of "Wayne's Richfield," a service station on the southwest corner of San Antonio and Atlantic. On one corner was Welch's, on another was Thrifty's and straight across the street was Lyman's.

My next-door neighbor, who delivered oil additives to local gas stations, told me Wayne's Richfield was about to open, and they were looking for two attendants. I went by and picked up my buddy Bob, and we headed up to place our job applications.

We were both hired on the spot, and we were going to be the nightshift employees, which was great for us since we were going to Poly. So the deal was $1.65 an hour and 10% commission on sales if we could sell at least $300.00 a month of oil, tires, batteries etc.

We were both "hustlers" and really liked our jobs. We were two blocks from home, our buddies hung out at Lyman's, and Russell's was right up the street. Bob worked 5-10 p.m., and I worked 7 'til midnight. We both worked 5-midnight on Saturdays.

Our friends would cruise over on Fridays and Saturdays: Joe, Tom, Mike and there were others like "trick truck" and "crispy critter"! We also had the benefit of working next door to "The Limit" nightclub, which brought its own unique perks!

At Wayne's we washed windows, checked under the hood and, if asked, checked tire pressure. When there was a big act at The Limit, such as Ike & Tina Turner, we would get plenty of business, as well as a lot of people asking to park at the station.

It didn't take us long to also realize the advantage of washing the windows of cars with girls in their mini skirts. This started a competition of who could get to the car first if it had girls in it. Sometimes we would be so obvious that we would both be washing the same side of the window.

However, the point of this was that Bob and I hustled to sell as much as we could so we would reach our bonus. We fell short the first month, but we both hit it our 2nd and third months. So we were surprised when Wayne told us that he had set our goals too low and was raising it to $400.00.

Confused and disappointed we set out to hit the $400.00 goal. After several months of trying, we figured out that it couldn't be done!

So Bob and I came up with our own strategy. Anytime we did something that was labor only, e.g. jumpstart a car, repair or change a tire, etc. we put the money in our pocket and didn't record the transaction if we were paid in cash.

This turned out to be great for us. We always had an extra few bucks in our pockets, which allowed us to eat more, especially several more Russell's burgers per week!

Wayne once mentioned the fact that our sales were down and said we needed to pick it up, but by this time we didn't care. I ended up working there until the middle of our senior year 1969! The hours were perfect for me: go to school, baseball practice or game until 5:00, grab a bite to eat and then work 7 to midnight.

Chapter 37 -- Rich's 40

In 1967 I was 16 and about the only kid in my neighborhood with a driver's license and a car. My car was a 1956 Chevy that I had big plans for. My best friend, Rich Skeber, came down to the house and wanted to know if I would drive him to Torrance to look at a 1940 Ford coupe.

I would have driven to look at any car, but I always liked the '40 Ford, as that was one of the cars my Dad had as a teenager and had customized. In fact, my Dad had to sell it when my Mom was pregnant with me in 1950.

Rich and I headed off to look at the car: a 1940 Ford coupe, gray primer with a 324 Olds engine, Cad La Salle transmission and '57 Olds rear end. Boy, it sure looked good.

The seller said we could take it out for a spin, but he wanted to hold Rich's driver's license. But Rich had no license, so he took mine and told us only I could drive it!

We took off in the '40 and drove it easy for a few blocks until Rich told me to jump on it so he could see what it could do. So I jumped on it, and we were both very impressed. Rich said in his excitement that it pulled the front wheels off the ground!

I told him I didn't think so, but we tried it several more times. Rich was convinced, we drove it back to the owner's house and Rich negotiated a deal for the coupe. He'd return the following day with the cash, and we'd drive it home.

Rich's dad agreed that he could buy the car, however, it had to stay in the garage until he got his driver's license, or unless I was the driver. This was great news for me. Rich didn't get his license for several months, and we drove it a lot with me at the wheel. It was great!

We also realized that the fenders at the front of the car were not bolted to the frame, so when I jumped on it, the fenders would raise up giving the effect of the wheels coming off the ground!

I was reminded of this today, as I was thinking about the New Year ahead and about Rich Skeber, whom I haven't seen since about 1970. And New Years Day is also Rich's birthday!

Chapter 38 – Trading for a Vette

In 1968, while I was working my night shift at Wayne's Richfield on the corner of San Antonio and Atlantic Ave., I heard the bell ring to let me know that a car had pulled up to one of the islands. As I headed out of the office door I saw a green Corvette.

As I approached I realized it was a guy we called "crispy critter." I don't remember his real name, but this was what I knew him as, an example of the cruel names that high school boys call someone behind their backs.

The story about him, as I was told, was that "crispy had stolen a motorcycle and was being pursued by the police when he crashed the bike, and it caught fire, and he was burned on his face.

Well, that day at Wayne's "crispy" hadn't come in for gas, he wanted to talk to me about my '56 Chevy. In 1968 I had done suspension work, tires and wheels, painted it a bright yellow by myself, and had just gotten it back from "Tia Juana" where I had installed a new diamond tuck interior.

It was fun to drive, looked great and was great for cruising the streets of Long Beach. The next step for me was to increase the car's performance. Did I go with a built 327 small block or a

396 or 427 Chevy big block? I hadn't made up my mind, but I also didn't have the money yet.

So "crispy" wanted to look at my new interior. After he spent 5 to 10 minutes checking out my car, he asks, "Would you like to trade your '56 for my '57 corvette"?

While I was surprised and intrigued by the idea, I told him that I needed a few days to think about it. He said, "Sure, let me know." After putting so much work into my car and considering the fact that I was the one who usually drove, the thought of giving up my car was tough to think about. However, the thought of having a sporty Corvette, and it still had room for my date, was winning the battle of "pros and cons."

So a couple of days later I saw my new Vette across the street at Lyman's and decided to drive over and give him my answer. "Yeah, I'll trade you for the Corvette!"

After a minute or so, he says, "$100.00 and your car and I'll make the trade." This was not what I expected to hear.

“Nope! Not going to do that!” was my answer, and I actually felt relieved. So that was it, no Vette, but I still had my '56 and the goal of improving the car’s power situation. I later installed a 427 Corvette big block in my car and decided that the new engine deserved a new paint color!

I still sometimes think that I should have ponied up the $100.00 and made the trade, but being a junior in high school, that was a lot of money! Besides, giving up the back seat probably wasn't a good idea.

Chapter 39 -- Baseball Cleats

My Mom and her new husband Ralph wanted to have all the family go camping in the Sierras. This was hard for me because of baseball, but I asked Herbold anyway.

"Can you be back to pitch on Sunday?" he asked.

"I'll be ready to go Sunday!"

So the family drove up in their white Cadillac, towing the dune buggy that Ralph had built in the backyard. My stepsister and her friend rode with me in the '56. So after four days in the mountains, I drove back to Long Beach on Saturday so I would make the game on Sunday.

Our game was an American Legion game, and it was in El Segundo. As I was dressing into my uniform, I looked around for my small equipment bag that I take to games that carried my glove, cleats, a baseball or two, and anything else that I typically took to our games. It wasn't in my room, checked the back porch, the garage and my car. Couldn't find it anywhere!

Well, I had another glove in my closet, but I needed cleats, and it was time to leave. I called my buddy Rich to see if they had any cleats I could borrow, the largest size they had. Rich said there are several pair in the garage, "Stop by and grab a pair."

So I jumped in my car, drove up the street to the Skeber's house and met Rich in the garage. The largest size they had were an old pair, size eleven, but they would have to do! When the family returned from the Sierras later in the week, I discovered that my little sister had loaded my bag into the Cadillac, just trying to help.

I drove to El Segundo arriving at 11:00, as expected by Herbold. I sat down on the bench and started putting on my cleats as Herbold walked by and asked if I'm ready to pitch today?

"Ready," I tell him, "feeling real good today."

However, as I was putting on the cleats I realized they hurt my feet worse than I expected. I wore a size 12 and have since 6th grade. The 11s are really tight!

But I went out and started playing catch with the rest of the guys. About 11:20, the guys took the field for infield practice, and I headed to the bullpen and start my warm-ups.

Looking across the field, we noticed only a couple of guys arriving for the other team. After our infield practice was over, the umpires arrived, but the other team had only seven players.

Herbold walked over to the other team and their coach was just now showing up. Their coach said that they would forego infield practice and assured us that at least two more players were on the way. Some had been surfing that morning, but "They'll be here!"

As Herbold was relaying this info to us he was cussing "Surfers!"

The umpire had them take the field. By then they only had eight players, so they decided to play with only two outfielders.

After our half of the inning was over, I headed to the mound and threw my eight warm-up pitches. Damn my feet hurt!

Their first batter stepped into the batter's box. I got the sign from my catcher, starting off with a fastball. Into my windup, and I let it fly!

"Crack!" My pitch sailed inside and hit the batter on the elbow, making a cracking sound. He fell to the ground grabbing his arm.

The coach and several players rushed out to check on him. After five minutes or so, they headed off to the dugout, grabbed their equipment and headed to their cars!

The umpire told Herbold and myself, "That's game!"

They thought he broke something, and the batter headed to the emergency room. The rest of the team didn't want to continue!

To say Herbold was pissed would be an understatement!

"Infield, get back on the field. Mosley, you get on the mound." Herbold then proceeded to hammer ground balls, line drives and everything else he can at us, just like in a game situation. Finally, he told us to bring it in, after what seemed like hours.

Most of us were pissed off now and just wanted to head home. I couldn't wait to get my cleats off. As I took my right shoe off, my sanitary sock was all bloody on the inside of my foot. The other shoe came off, no blood.

Herbold saw my foot and said, "Well, I guess you had an excuse," and walked away. I walked to my car, and pulled off my socks. An eyelet from the borrowed cleats had worn a round hole into my foot! Geez, it hurt!

I had that scar for almost 20 years!

Chapter 40 -- Rich's Garage

In February of 1968 we were starting to work out on the Poly football field for the upcoming Poly baseball season. We would exercise, run and then the pitchers would throw softballs to build up our arm strength. Later when our actual practices started, we would take the bus to Silverado Park every afternoon, since Poly did not have a field. Our home field for games was Blair Field.

My friend Rich was working on his '40 Ford coupe, painting the dash, window frames and was replacing the rear windows with blue Plexiglas. When I got home from school, I would grab a snack and head up to his house and give him a hand. This particular afternoon after hanging out for a while, his mom called him in for dinner.

As Rich climbed out of the '40, he quickly slammed the car door, smashing my thumb, the thumb on my pitching hand! Damn did that hurt, as blood started coming out from beneath my thumbnail. As I clutched my thumb, the radio was playing "Hello Stranger" by Barbara Lewis.

Thinking my baseball season may be over before it started, I was really "pissed off" as I headed home. I soaked my hand in ice water all evening as my thumb continued to throb. At school the next day I told Coach Herbold what had happened, and he said just continue to practice and start throwing again when I could. After a few weeks, with my black thumb nail taped up I could throw without too much pain.

We had started playing practice games and we had one at Bellflower High School on Friday afternoon. On the bus ride to the game I told Herbold that I thought I could pitch. Coach Herbold was planning on using several pitchers that day and that I would pitch the last two innings.

As I warmed up during the game, my thumb throbbed a little more each time I threw a pitch. My thumbnail was holding on by one side only, and I needed to keep it taped to hold it in place. As I walked to the mound in the bottom of the sixth, we had a two run lead.

I had barely thrown a baseball since we started practicing, so when I took the mound my control wasn't the best. I walked a couple of batters, and they scored a run. In the seventh inning as I started to pitch to their first batter, he pointed out to his coach and the umpire that I had tape on my pitching hand.

The umpire told me that I had to remove the tape if I was going to continue to pitch. So I removed the tape and began pitching to the batter. Each pitch I threw now caused my nail to sort of flap as though it was going to be ripped off.

Well, I was having a problem throwing strikes and with two outs they scored two runs to beat us. They we thrilled to beat the "great" Poly team. I walked over to the bench, my thumb throbbing and mad that I had lost the game.

As I was taking off my cleats, the batter that had asked the umpire to have me remove the tape came over to shake my hand and said, "Nice game!" I told him to kiss my ass, and he apparently didn't like that.

So an argument between the two teams ensued, and the

Bellflower coach was nose to nose with Coach Herbold, and I was then right behind Herbold. The Bellflower coach said something to the effect that I had said, "F**k off," and that there was no place for that kind of talk.

Well, I hadn't said that, and I reached over Herbold's shoulder, grabbed the coach by his shirt and told him his player was a liar.

Herbold pushed me away, restored order and had us grab our gear and get on the bus.

When we took the bus on the following Monday afternoon to Silverado Park for practice, Herbold read a letter that stated that Bellflower High School would no longer play Poly in any kind of sports.

I was sorry about what had happened, but I often played angry. At 16, I was an angry young man, and playing for Coach Herbold didn't help.

As I sat on the bus the song "Hello Stranger" played in my head – and to this day when I get upset, or things aren't going right, that song always pops into my head.

Chapter 41 -- The Carport

Dylan was playing on my Muntz four-track tape player as I was driving down Artesia Blvd. in my '56 Chevy. It was about 10:00 p.m., and Rich was looking outside the passenger window trying to spot a car that he'd heard about.

Between Clark and Downey on the north side of the street were several old houses tucked away in the over-grown trees.

"I think I saw it!" shouted Rich. "Quick, turn around and go back!"

As I turned the '56 around, I slowly headed back up Artesia. As I approached the houses, I slowed to a stop. Next to this old house, parked in a carport, half hidden by an over-grown tree, was the front-end of a 1940 Ford.

Rich rolled down the window and exclaimed, "Looks like a good one!"

After straining to see more of the '40 from my car, I put the transmission into first and headed back up Artesia. "We need to come back by tomorrow and check it out further."

So began a couple of weeks of our new pattern. Anytime we were out and about, Rich wanted to cruise back by the gray '40 parked in the carport. We did this possibly a dozen times before we got up the nerve to stop and knock on the door.

While Rich knocked, I quickly made my way around the car. No engine or upholstery. Inside the '40 Ford coupe were two black bucket seats, probably out of a Volkswagen.

When no one answered the door, Rich joined me in checking out the car. It wasn't gray, but an ugly dull white. The body was really straight; the grille looked like it'd been recently re-chromed.

"We should probably get out of here," I said. Rich and I climbed back into my Chevy and off we went, vowing to return.

It was probably two weeks later, on what now had become part of our routine, that we drove by in the early evening, and it looked like someone was home.

Stopping in front of the driveway, Rich headed to the door while I sat and listened to the Animals Greatest Hits.

Shortly thereafter, Rich went into the small house and remained inside for about ten minutes or so. When the door opened and Rich re-appeared, he almost ran toward me and my Chevy.

"He might sell, has freshly chromed bumpers and other parts in the house! No engine and he'd sell it for 100 dollars."

This was great news for Rich, who had been missing his last '40, since he sold it six months earlier. This would make a fantastic project!

Rich's Dad, however, wasn't as enthusiastic as we were. His large gold Plymouth sedan would have to be parked in the driveway again while Rich took up the garage space with another 1940 Ford coupe.

Still, we cruised by the house on Artesia, music blaring from my tape player, but then it became less frequent.

Now, I had always wanted a '40 Ford coupe, and the thought of me buying the coupe was starting to keep me up at night. I hadn't yet stuck a lot of money into my '56 Chevy.

So by then, every time we went by, in my mind it was more for me than it was for Rich. However, I didn't have the resources to own both cars.

"I could buy the '40, but it would sit until I could sell my Chevy," I reasoned, "but if I sell the Chevy, then I don't have transportation until the '40 is drivable." Such was the dilemma of an 11th grade student in the winter 1967.

"Well, let's drive by the '40 again," Rich said.

"Sure, let's go!" I agreed.

Well, that was the last time we headed down Artesia looking for the '40. While listening to the Buffalo Springfield and Mr. Soul, we looked over and the '40 was gone! The house looked empty, and an ugly couch and chair sat on the carport.

"Damn, I should have bought it!" we both said.

Chapter 42 -- Infield Practice
Blair Field 1968

Our infield warm-up before a game was normally a show -- a great thing to watch. Perfection! The baseball scouts that came to our Poly games usually showed up early to watch, we were that good.

On this particular day, things didn't go as they normally did. I remember we were playing Lakewood High School. Herbold had the infield and outfield on the field with the starters and non-starters. Basically, there were two players at each position. Herbold would hit the ball to left field yelling, "Two." The player would get to the ball and fire it into second base.

Next, he'd hit to the outfielders, yelling, "Home." The first ball that came into home bounced to the starting catcher who caught and gestured tagging a runner trying to score.

Then Herbold lined one to the extra fielder who made his throw to home. Our second string catcher, Dean, attempted to make the catch but the ball skidded off his glove.

Then he hit it to the centerfielders and the starting catcher again made the play. The next fielder fired it home, and again the ball bounced off Dean's glove.

Herbold yelled, "Hold on to the ball!" Well, after about five or six throws to home plate that bounced off Dean's glove, Herbold is pissed and yelled, "Again!"

He lined one to left again and yelled at Dean, "You take all these throws." Two more scoot away from the catcher as the throws came in.

Herbold yelled, "Home" to the centerfielders as he lined the ball over second base. The throw was slightly up the third base line as Dean started to move toward it.

Herbold then pushed Dean out of the way at the last minute and caught the ball himself barehanded and made a motion to tag the runner.

"Again," he yelled and lined it again to center. Again, the throw came to the plate, and again Dean had it go off his glove!

Now some of the Lakewood parents are yelling things at Herbold. Herbold then lined one to right field yelling, "Home."

As Dean moved toward the ball, again Herbold shoved him out of the way and made the play himself barehanded, and then he yelled, "Tag him" as he motions toward home plate.

Now the Lakewood fans are really getting on Herbold! Herbold lined another to right, the throw coming home and Herbold again pushed Dean out of the way, catching the ball several feet behind the third base foul line.

Herbold then dove forward landing on his stomach, and holding the ball in both hands he started pounding the dirt and yelling "TAG HIM, TAG HIM, TAG HIM!" Herbold got up, dirt all over the front of his uniform, and the Lakewood fans are now going crazy!

I was watching all this thinking, what the hell just took place? Herbold un-phased by anything going on in the stands finished up with the infield, putting on our normal show!

Dean's confidence was now shaken and in the next several practices he couldn't throw the ball straight! Even when he was catching batting practice, he couldn't throw the ball back to the pitcher!

One bounced, one went to the right, the next one over the

pitchers head and into centerfield. Dean had a really good arm and could throw hard. To try and compensate for his lack of accuracy, he started throwing the ball even harder!

A week or two went by and Herbold decided to pitch Ray, with Dean starting behind the plate. During the game Dean's throws are going everywhere except into Ray's glove. We had the game well in hand so Herbold left him behind the plate hoping he'd work through this.

The opposition got a runner on first late in the game and I'm certain because of Dean's throwing problems, the runner decided to try and steal second. Ray delivered a strike to the plate as everyone yelled, "He's going!"

Ray dropped to a knee, almost to a squatting position, to give Dean room to throw to second. Dean came out of his crouch and rifled the ball toward second. Thud, the ball drilled Ray in the rib cage, as the ball never made it more than three feet off the ground!

Ray lay there on the mound in pain, the runner was into second easily, and I'm not sure if Dean ever played in a game again!

Chapter 43 --"I Can Catch You With a Kleenex"

This was another one of Herbold's sayings. Others he had were, "I could call that with Braille," and "That's a bat, not the Christian Science Monitor!" We heard these all the time. He had lots of them.

Since Poly had no baseball field, we took a bus every day and practiced at Silverado Park, and our home games were at Blair Field. On the bus ride to practice we would receive a schedule of what and when things were going to happen: Play catch, 3:15 to 3:25, pitchers run in the outfield 3:25 to 3:45, etc.

This particular day we were playing a "simulated game." Pitchers would pitch as if we were playing an actual game, and the batters would run the bases if they got a hit or walked.

Gary was a left-handed pitcher who threw a lot of big breaking curveballs because he didn't have much of a fastball. Well, Gary was on the mound and throwing a lot of curves to the hitters, and Herbold yelled, "Throw some fastballs."

Gary tossed a few and Herbold yelled, "Harder!"

Gary fired several more, and Herbold yelled, "Harder!" Several more fastballs and Herbold yelled, "I could catch you with a Kleenex!"

Herbold was now standing near the catcher as Gary fired

more fastballs. Herbold then told the catcher to move, and he crouched down behind the plate.

"Throw me a fastball," he yelled. Gary fired one home, and coach Herbold caught it barehanded!

"Harder" he yelled. Gary again threw his fastball to the plate, and Herbold again caught it barehanded!

"Mosley," get out there!" I took the mound, threw a few warm-up pitches and practice continued. As I was pitching through the line-up, I then became the target of Herbold's attention.

"Mosley, you can throw harder than that! Let it loose!"

So I start throwing a little harder. A few more banters and a few more fastballs, and I get the "I can catch you with a Kleenex!"

Now, I threw a lot harder than Gary, and I was just hoping he was going to try and catch me barehanded. Sure enough, Herbold got behind the plate without a glove and yelled, "Throw me a fastball." I reared back and let one fly!

Herbold reached at the pitch, but let it whiz past his hand and past his ear.

"That a boy, Mosley, good fastball! New pitcher," Herbold yelled!

Chapter 44 -- Blair Field 1968 Moore League Baseball

We had a great baseball team in 1968. The hard work of the previous two years was paying dividends. When our team took the field before a game, the scouts were there to watch. We were a well-oiled machine, and the infield and outfield drills were quite a show.

I don't remember who we were playing this particular afternoon, but I will never forget what took place. I thought it was great at the time, and one of the moments that stand out during my time with Poly Baseball.

Herbold was our coach, and he would stand at the top of the steps of the dugout during the games. And he yelled. I mean he really yelled! A lot!

One of his favorite words of the day was "HORSESHIT!" I can still hear that echoing throughout Blair Field. This particular game I was not pitching, just watching from the dugout, and listening to Herbold.

About the middle of the game with two outs and our team in the field, the opposing batter drilled a long fly ball to right field. Our right fielder Roland usually played kind of shallow, because he was fast. In fact, most of our team was fast!

Well this drive to right was sailing way over Roland's head. Roland turned his back to home plate, sprinted toward the outfield wall, turned and raised his glove to make the catch. However, the ball hit the heel of the glove and fell to the ground with the batter easily reaching second base.

Well, Herbold started in, "How could you drop a ball that hits your glove?" "That's horseshit!"

The next batter made the third out and our team is headed toward the dugout. Herbold was now out by the third base line and he was giving Roland an ear full, all the way from right field and into the dugout!

Roland took a seat next to us on the bench and pulled off one of his cleats, throwing it across the dugout! Herbold saw this and came down the steps into the dugout -- and he was seething!

He yelled at Roland, "Take off that other cleat and you're through!"

Well, Roland removed his other cleat and fired it across the dugout!

Herbold yelled, "Get out!"

Now to get to the dressing room at Blair, Roland had to walk past where Herbold was now standing. Picking up his glove Roland walked toward Herbold who was now yelling again!

As Roland approached Herbold he dropped his glove, grabbed Herbold by the shirt of his uniform and shoved him against the wall yelling, "Listen, fat man, you ever yell at me again, I'll kick your ass!"

Roland then released Herbold and headed off to the showers. Herbold turned his attention back to the game. We sat in silence for several minutes and figured we'd seen Roland for the last time in a Poly uniform.

A couple of days later we are practicing at Silverado Park

and Roland was approaching the field, glove in hand, ready to go. Herbold said that he and Roland had worked things out.

Herbold said, "I may have over-reacted. I don't think another outfielder could have even gotten to the ball."

We went on to win Moore League and advanced to the final game of the CIF Championship, where we lost a game that we should have won ...

Chapter 45 -- For the Love of the Game

I grew up wanting to be a baseball player. The second time my new friend Rich came to my door, he gave me a small booklet, "Spaulding's Guide to Playing Baseball." I still have that book today, stuck away with my baseball cards.

I read that book cover to cover several times, reading the text and studying the pictures and diagrams. Rich and I would play catch and then "pickle" in the backyard. We soon rounded up a couple of other kids, and then we would go to the park and play "over-the-line." This is a game that we would play well into high school.

In third grade I tried out for the Browns of the Kiwanis T-Shirt League where I became their starting first baseman for the next two seasons. I was only about nine at the time, and I couldn't get enough of the game.

I was collecting baseball cards, listening to Vin and Jerry announce the Dodger games, checking the box scores in the Press Telegram and watching any baseball movie that came on television. My favorites were "The Babe Ruth Story" and "The Winning Team" about pitcher Grover Cleveland Alexander. There were other baseball movies about Lou Gerhig, Jackie Robinson and Dizzy Dean. I watched them all any time they were on.

I went on to play two years in the Long Beach Elks League, the Rotary League, and three years for Hughes Junior High, Connie Mack, American Legion and then three years at Poly.

When I graduated from Hughes, Coach Herbold asked me if I wanted to play that summer for his Long Beach Blues team. They were a Connie Mack team, and the caliber of play was high. Most the players were several years older, but I was thrilled to accept the challenge. I had always played first base and had just starting pitching.

Pitching was now my position, like it or not. But this was also when the game changed for me. I learned a lot about pitching and the game of baseball. Herbold had a saying, "You don't play baseball, you work it!"

Well, we did work it at Poly, and we were successful. We won Moore League in '68, my junior year, but lost in the CIF championship game. After that game, Herbold announced that he wouldn't be back for our senior year. Instead he was going to coach Lakewood, one of our hated rivals.

That summer I was without a team. For the first time since I was eight, I didn't play any summer ball! The thrill seemed to be gone, and so was the fun.

My senior year, we finished right behind Lakewood and Millikan who had tied for first. I led the league with low ERA and was asked to pitch at LB State.

Last night I watched a movie with Kevin Costner, "For the Love of the Game." I stumbled across this movie a few years back and now cannot turn it off whenever it is on.

Costner plays an aging major league pitcher who recounts his meeting a gal and their relationship of the last few years. He is recounting these events while pitching a game. It is something that fascinates me, because that is what pitching is, it's mental.

When I started pitching full time, it took away the fun of the sport for me. I would do what Costner is doing in this movie. When you're on the mound, you think about what you know about the batter. Do you throw inside, high or low, can he hit a curve, how many outs, what inning, what's the score, are there runners on base, what is Herbold yelling!

I would look in to get the sign from my catcher and then think, "Geeze, I have to work tonight!"

The next inning, or next game, as I threw every pitch, I might be thinking that this umpire is not giving me the outside corner, and my step-sisters are going to be at the house all weekend, and that sucks! I hope my boss left me money in the desk drawer, because I have a date tonight, as I just gave up a double! Two on, two outs, 2-2 count on the batter, and as I go into my stretch, I'm thinking, my parents haven't seen me play since I was in eighth grade!

Our last game at Poly was against Millikan at Blair Field and their second baseman was coming to the plate in the seventh and final inning. He was what we called "a hot dog," and I'd been pitching against him for years. The catcher gave me a sign for a fastball inside, and I believed he was thinking the same thing as me, "Hit this guy!"

Well, I threw it high and under his chin, and he hit the dirt! Our coach, and I don't even remember his name, calls "time" and heads to the mound.

"Are you going to hit him?" he asks.

"Just as hard as I can," I replied.

"I thought so; I'm making a pitching change!"

And I was done. Little did I know that I'd choose to never pitch again ...

Chapter 46 -- Spring of 1969

Graduation is approaching and I cannot wait. Just get me out of here!

My long-time girlfriend had moved on from me, and I dated a couple of girls that I liked. One girl I took out to dinner, and then we drove to Hollywood to see a movie. Fun night.

I pulled up to her house around midnight and walked her to her front door in Bixby Knolls. As we were walking to the door, I was thinking, "Should I try to kiss her on our first date?"

As we reached the front door she turned to me, planted a really nice kiss on my lips and said, "Please call me. I had a really good time!"

"I will," and I turned to walk back to my car.

Wow, that was fun! I started my car and drove to Lyman's to see if any of the guys are there. Normal procedure.

Well, I waited a few days and decided to give her a call. She answered and said that she was so glad that I called. I have something to tell you!

"I had a really good time last week. However, my boyfriend and I have patched things up."

"Well, that sucks," I said to myself after I hanged up the phone.

My Mom wanted me to call a girl I went to kindergarten with. Mom and her mom had stayed friends all these years and "She's not dating anyone right now." Well, why not? She was pretty cute as I remembered her in kindergarten. I gave her a call, and we made a date. She lived in Torrance and went to South High. I drove to Torrance and picked her up and off we went. We grabbed a bite to eat and ended up at the miniature golf course and batting cages. She was very cute, really nice and easy to talk with.

The one thing that bothered me a bit was that she was only 5 feet tall! I thought, "Feels really tiny, I'm 6 feet 2!" I discovered that she was a cheerleader and was the Homecoming Queen! All good things.

We dated several more times, a movie, dinner, and one evening I took her to Lyman's. On our next date she wanted stay in. Her Dad was gone and, "We'll be alone!" This sounded great! We had a really good evening, but something kind of bothered me ... She made me a cake!

As I left her that night and made the long drive back to Long Beach I kept thinking, "I had a great time, but she made me a cake! She's really cute, but she's so tiny! She wants to get serious! Made me a cake! So tiny! Kind of really makes me nervous!" I never called her again. I'm not sure why, other than those two reasons.

Prom was approaching, and I didn't have a date! Well, my best friend those days was Bob, and he'd been dating Beth. Beth told me I should call her friend Melissa. "Melissa might be looking for a date to the prom, and you two should really get along!"

Well, I knew Melissa. We had Government with Mr. Jameson in 10th grade. It was during the first lunch period, which my girlfriend at that time had! So I would occasionally approach Melissa, who took attendance for Mr. Jameson, and ask her to mark me present in class so I could go eat lunch with my girlfriend. She always did, and it was really cool! On another time for the Sphinx Dance in 11th grade my girlfriend wanted to double date. It was with Melissa and her date.

Well, I called Melissa and asked her to the senior prom, and she accepted! We were going to double date with Bob and Beth, have dinner at Mr. C's and then go to the Lafayette Hotel for the prom.

A week or so later was the senior picnic. I went to school for attendance, and as everyone walked to the front of school to get on the buses for the ride to El Dorado Park, I was headed to my car and planned on going anywhere but to the picnic.

As I got near the school entrance there was the cute and very popular Melissa. She walked toward me to see if I wanted to go to picnic with her. "Sure," I said, and we climbed aboard a bus for the ride to the park. She had made a terrific lunch!

We spent the day off away from all the activities and got to know each other. It turned out we had a lot in common. Her family spent most of their vacations fishing in the Sierras a few miles away from where we vacationed when my Dad was living.

We knew a lot of the same people. She was president of her sorority, but I decided not to hold that against her! It turned out to be a terrific day and the beginning of a really fun summer. After the prom, we did Grad Nite together, flew to Catalina for the day, went to Lion's Drag Strip, horseback riding in Big Bear and the best was a week at Convict Lake camping and fishing.

I took her to a party right after school was out to meet a bunch of my friends. Turned out that she knew a few of the gals, a couple had been in her sorority. I introduced her to "screwdrivers" that night and ended up carrying her for most of the party. She was a hit!

I'm not sure what happened to Melissa. I heard she's been married for 48 years, or so! It's been quite the adventure, so far.

Picking Melissa Up Before The Prom

At The Poly High School Prom 1969

Grad Nite-Disneyland 1969

Melissa at Lion's Drag Strip and in Big Bear
Summer 1969

Chapter 47 -- Work or School

I spent the most of the summer of '69 hanging out with Melissa and friends. As fall approached I decided that I was not going to play baseball at Long Beach State. In fact, I decided I was not going to go to school in the fall. I was getting close to getting my '56 finished and back on the road. I needed money and a job.

The guys that had cars that I hung out with had a kind of "mentor," Tom McKee. Tom had graduated from Poly in 1966 and had an age advantage on the rest of us. My best friend Bob had heard that Tom was working at the Fiat warehouse, so Bob went and applied for a job and was hired. The pay was pretty good, so I went and applied for a position and was also hired. How cool was this, three of us working at the same place.

The job was good, working with car parts every day. Fiat would ship parts via ships from Italy to Long Beach and then truck the parts to our warehouse. We would unpack and place the parts on the shelves. At the same time, the office would take orders from the Fiat dealers in southern California, and we would take the orders and then pull the parts, tag and bag them and deliver them to shipping.

Tom got promoted to the office, and Mike, another of the "car gang," filled that warehouse position. To keep ourselves entertained, we would make "tape balls" and sneak around and throw it hard at an unsuspecting victim in the next aisle. This was a blast, because I was good!

Once I fired a long shot at one of the guys, missed him and it rolled through the legs of a corporate big wig as he came out of the office. Luckily, he didn't see where it came from.

There were several "older" men who worked in the warehouse also. Abe was old and grumpy, and then Vic, who we would wake up every morning as he slept in his car in the parking lot.

Vic had another job, graveyard shift, and then he would sleep for an hour or so in his car before doing his eight-hour shift at Fiat! Vic was cool, and we left him alone.

However, it was fun to mess with Abe. As he walked through the warehouse with his cart pulling parts, a tape ball to the back was fun. If he left his cart unattended for a moment, we would hide parts he had already pulled or hide his paperwork. Great stuff when you're 18.

Of course, there was the office queen. She was very cute, blonde, about 30 years old. On Fridays she usually wore a see-through blouse and a black bra. That's all I remember about her.

As the months went by Mike decided to quit. Bob sold his '55 Chevy and bought a used motorcycle and a Chevy van. Bob's van was cool, but he didn't like to drive it because of the blind spots on each side. I became the van driver when we went places.

I found a 120 Kawasaki for $50.00, stripped off the lights, fenders and speedometer, installed a new rear sprocket and knobby tire, and Bob and I had a new hobby. Bob and I started going to Palmdale, camping and riding our dirt bikes.

Bob quit his job at Fiat and was encouraging me to do the same. I was holding on so I could finish my car. Dennis was hired to take Bob's place, the fifth member of the "gang" to get hired.

Tom finally had enough of working in the office, and he abruptly quit. We always ate our lunches outside in the parking lot, and as I walked outside to eat one Friday afternoon, Bob was sitting there in his van.

I walked up to the window and Bob said, "Let's go!"

"Go where?" I asked.

"Palmdale, let's beat the traffic. I went by your house, loaded up your bike, sleeping bag and the ice chest is full! Let's go!"

"I can't just quit!"

Bob told me, "Sure you can, let's go!"

"Follow me home so I can drop off my sedan delivery," I told him.

And we were off! A week or so later I received my last check in the mail, and they let Dennis go. I guess they figured he'd quit next!

Tom's Garage In 1969
Tom McKee, Mike Williams, Me, Rich Skeber
Joe Jarreau, Dennis Donaldson

Chapter 48 -- For What It's Worth

In the spring of 1970, my best friend Bob and I decided to drive to the Sierras the week after opening day of the trout season. We threw our gear into the back of my '55 Chevy sedan delivery and headed out late Friday night.

Driving most of the night across the Mojave Desert, I was exhausted by the time I pulled off the road in a turnout along side of Rock Creek, just south of Mammoth Lakes. We climbed into our sleeping bags in the back and went to sleep. I awoke as I heard the back door open and then close.

Cold and still tired, I decided I would let Bob do his thing. Minutes later the back opened again, and Bob climbed back into his sleeping bag. Now I'm wide-awake, and I ask Bob, "Did you have to pee?"

Bob replied that he was climbing down the hill to the creek, slid on the loose rock and fell.

"I tried to catch myself by grabbing the large granite boulder as I slid, but it tore the skin off my finger tips, and it's cold outside! It's safer in here," he said.

We laid in our bags for a while waiting for the sun to rise

and the temperature to warm a bit. We finally got up and decided to drive back down the road to Tom's Place for breakfast.

After we ate, we drove to Mammoth for groceries and then back to Convict Lake where we selected a campsite. We fished during the days and then would drive to Hot Creek to soak and enjoy a few libations.

On our last evening we bought a six-pack and a bottle of wine and were off again to Hot Creek. This time of year there were only a few people there, and they would leave soon after dark. As we walked down the trail to the hot pools, we saw a truck dropping down to the creek on the opposite side of the creek. We could see these two guys open the tailgate and start unloading firewood.

By the time we reached the bottom they had a fire going on the bank of the creek. No one else was there, and as we approached the fire we saw two guys about our age standing by the fire and opening a beer!

"Hey guys, can we share the fire?"

"Sure, and have a beer," we're told.

"Have our own, but thanks!"

They introduced themselves as one of them walked to the truck and turned on the tape player.

"I'm Bob and that's Chuck cranking up the music!"

"That's crazy!" I said! "I'm Chuck and this here is Bob!"

The tape player started blaring "For What It's Worth." This is one of my favorite tapes by the Buffalo Springfield. We enjoyed a couple of beers by the fire with our new friends Chuck and Bob and then stepped into the geysers of hot creek with our bottle of wine.

At hot creek over the years the tradition was bathing suits and families during the day, and the suits would come off after dark. Since there were only the four guys, we elected to forego tradition.

About an hour into our soak, we saw three people coming down the steep trail from the parking lot. As they get closer we see that it's three ladies wearing ski clothes. It was the first week of May, and they were still skiing at Mammoth.

The three ladies approached the fire and asked, "Can we share your fire?"

"Sure, help yourself," the other Bob says to the gals. They dropped their bags and one of them pulled out a bottle of wine.

Wow, these gals were really good looking, we observed, were probably in their 30s, I surmised. They passed their wine around between them for ten minutes or so, and then the unimaginable happened.

The three gals, while standing in the light of the fire, stepped out of their ski clothes, and then took off their bras and panties!

The four of us guys, two Bobs and two Chucks, stared in disbelief. The three beautiful gals were now standing naked with the fire glowing off their bodies as they made their way into the water.

They offered us some wine, and we all had a taste or two. Not long after they entered the water, the other Chuck and Bob climbed out of the creek, threw some more wood onto the fire, hollered, "Goodbye," and headed their four-wheel drive Dodge up the hill and out of sight.

The three gals were now engulfed in their own conversations, so Bob and I decided it was time for us to leave as well.

So it was back to camp, and then we headed back to Long Beach in the morning.

Oh, and we did catch a lot of trout!

Chapter 49 -- VW Bus

In the spring of 1970 I was approaching my 19th birthday. I'd finished my '56 Chevy with new green paint, a 427 Corvette engine, and I've run it several times at Lions Drag Strip. I bought it from my Grandma after it had been stolen and stripped. Since I purchased this car, every extra dollar I earned was put into the car. Often times I knew what my next three paychecks were going for: a manifold, carburetors, headers or wheels and tires.

So after towing it home one night after running at Lions with my '55 Chevy sedan delivery, and it not wanting to start the next morning, I decided it was time to sell.

So I placed an ad in the *Press-Telegram* and then spent the next couple of days trying to start the car. I tried everything I knew, but it would not start. If I rolled it down the driveway and popped the clutch, it fired right up and ran great!

So Friday night I got a call from someone who sounded really interested in the car, and he made an appointment to see it the following day at 10:00 a.m. Melissa and I worked on the car late into the night washing, cleaning it and trying to get it to start. However, it was just not happening! I decided to make up some kind of excuse for the problem and hoped that he'd be OK with that.

Well, this guy showed up at 10:00 with three other guys to look at the '56. It was parked in front of my house and really looked good. They checked the car out from front to rear and they loved it!

"Can I drive it?" he asked.

"No, but I'll take you for a ride!"

He said, "That's fine, let's go!"

I decided I'll have to think fast when it won't start. I climbed into my seat, and he climbed in next to me. I turn on the electric fuel pump, let it build pressure and turn the key. It fired right up! I'm speechless! It actually started right up!

So I put it in first and headed out. I gave the guy a thrill ride through the neighborhood.

When I got back to the house, the guy said, "I'll take it." With no dickering whatsoever, he paid my price in hundred dollar bills. I handed over the pink slip, they piled in -- and naturally it doesn't start!

I told him that it occasionally did this. Satisfied with the explanation we pushed it, he popped the clutch and off they went! Never saw the car again!

I decided to buy a new dirt bike. I walked in to the Yamaha dealer and walked out with a new bike.

My next purchase was going to be something more practical -- something that I wouldn't have to work on. So off I went to Circle Volkswagen, and I ordered a new VW Bus, perfect for heading out and seeing America.

So I gave them $50.00 to order it, but since I didn't have any credit, I needed a co-signer. Well, I figured this should not be a problem, and I asked my Mom. Well, she had remarried and told me that I would have to ask Ralph.

Much to my surprise Ralph says, "NO!" He had never had a

new car and figured I should not have a new car before him. Well, I've never been much for "No's" and decided to ask my Grandmother. (My Dad's Mom) So I asked her if she would co-sign for my loan and, after my guarantees that I'll make the payments, she agreed.

Several weeks later I got the call that my bus was in, and I could come pick it up. I called Grandma, and she agreed to meet me there in the morning on her way to work.

Well, we went into the salesman's office and he started asking her questions and filling out the loan app: Name, address, place of employment. Then he asked where she banks and her account numbers, etc.

Grandma told him she was not going to give him that information, that it was "none of your business," she told him. Wow, I didn't expect this!

Grandma asked me, "How much is the vehicle and how much am I borrowing?" So I tell her, "$3,200.00 for the bus, and I'm putting a $1,000.00 down!"

"So you need $2,200.00?"

"Yes," I replied as she started digging into her purse. I assumed she was looking for her checkbook when she pulled out a bundle of cash wrapped in a large rubber band.

She started pulling out hundred dollar bills and stacking them on the desk.

"Grandma, I don't want to borrow the money from you. I really appreciate this, but I need to establish credit."

"I'm not giving this guy any more information, so let me just pay for it, and you can pay me back later."

The salesman finally spoke up and asked her if she would just sign the application, and he wouldn't ask her any more questions.

Grandma signed the app, put her cash back in her purse and said, "Well, I've got to get to work. Bring it by tomorrow morning, and I'll fix you breakfast!" And off she went.

The salesman told me everything was great, and then asked me, "Does grandma always carry around that kind of cash in her purse? I'll bet she had $10,000.00!"

"I don't know," I told him. "But she always has 'ice cream money' for us grandkids!" So I drove out in my bus, took it over to show my Grandma in the morning and had my favorite breakfast of pancakes and bacon ...

My ’56 Chevy when I sold it….Spring 1970

Showing Grandma Katie My New Bus 1970

Chapter 50 -- Parks Texaco

In the summer of 1970, I was going through the process of joining the Electrical Union. This was a process that, when I signed up, I thought would take a month or so. However, reality had now set in, and by then I knew it was a nine-month process from start to finish, consisting of a series of different tests and interviews.

I had quit my steady job at Fiat Motors to spend time riding dirt bikes, camping and mainly having a good time. But I was beginning to run short of the cash I had put away and needed something to tide me over until I would start my apprenticeship.

Having plenty of service station experience and growing up in Bixby Knolls, I decided that I would seek employment with Parks Texaco. It was close and seemed like a very clean and friendly station just a few blocks up on Long Beach Blvd. So I cleaned up, put on a nice shirt and drove to the station and filled out an application.

When I returned home several hours later, Mom said I had a message to call Parks Texaco. I gave them a call and was told I had the job if I would be willing to work 5:00 p.m. until midnight. I said that was perfect for me and was told to come by the following day and pick up my uniforms.

I was pretty excited to start work, and when I picked up the uniforms, I was told that I needed to drive over and meet my manager, and he would give me my schedule.

"Drive over where?" I asked, while standing in the office of the station. You'll be working at our station on the corner of Anaheim and Alamitos. Wow, I thought I would be working here in Bixby Knolls!

I drove to my new station and was told I could start tonight and that there would be a guy that would teach me the ropes. When I showed up for work, I learned I was replacing the guy that was showing me what was up.

The office and shop bays were closed and locked during the night shift, and I was to work out of a small booth right there on the island.

"Here is the cash box, your keys and a .38 revolver in case anyone tries to rob you!" he told me. And then this guy was gone.

I worked there for about three months. Then the Union called me, and I started my apprenticeship on Aug. 3rd. But I actually enjoyed working there. There was never a dull moment, especially on Friday and Saturday nights.

I was amused at the "guys" who would pull into the station in a nice Rivera or Coupe de Ville and then ask for a dollar's worth of gas when they had a wad of cash in their pockets. (Gas was about 33 cents a gallon at the time.)

The outfits these guys wore fascinated me: Three piece suits, usually orange, yellow or lime green, white belt and shoes and often a hat. There was the occasional "street walker" who came by asking to use the restroom, but my favorites were the guys that would ask for change for a twenty and then ask for some specific bills. Then they would hand you back a ten while they were hoping to confuse and short-change you. Being good at math and good with money I always thought this was a fun and amusing interaction.

Just a couple customers stood out. One guy came in and ordered a dollar's worth of gas, but then asked for his windshield to be cleaned, then asked if I'd check the oil, and then asked if I'd check the air pressure in his tires.

He really enjoyed ordering me around, and I went through the motions of half of his requests. I then went to the pump, removed the gas cap from behind the license plate and put a gallon of gas in his tank and the rest I put on the ground under his car. I hoped he didn't get far and ran out of gas unexpectedly!

My favorite customer came "flying down Alamitos" heading south, pulled into the station and came to a sliding stop on the far island. As I came up to his window, he said, "Fill it up! I'm in a hurry!"

I walked to the rear of the Mustang, removed the gas cap and started pumping gas into the tank. As I was holding the nozzle, I had only put in four or five gallons, he started up the engine, put it in gear, burned rubber across the island and headed back out onto Alamitos. I stood there holding the gas cap in one hand and the nozzle in the other.

A minute or two later two police cars, sirens blaring, came racing through the intersection. This turned out to be a very entertaining couple of months.

Me And Grandma Katie-My Favorite Picture Of The Two Of Us

Chapter 51 -- Grandma Katie

I mentioned my Grandma in a previous story, "VW Bus." She was going to co-sign for my first loan, but wouldn't give out any bank information on the credit application, and then proceeded to pull out about $10,000.00 that she had in her purse!

My Grandma was born in the hills of Tennessee in December of 1913. She was born premature, and they didn't think she would survive. They kept her in the warming oven in the wood-burning cook stove those first few days. They were poor sharecroppers, growing cotton, and she often talked about picking cotton during her childhood and being able to pick as much as the adults.

They eventually moved to Oklahoma where she met and married my Grandfather and had two kids, my Dad and my Aunt. She and my grandfather operated a small dairy farm with 32 cows, milking them by hand twice a day. They would divorce in the late '30s, and they both ended up migrating to Long Beach.

My Grandma ended up living in North Long Beach, renting a small bungalow with her two young children. She took a job as a waitress in downtown at the bus station. She would walk from their house near Artesia to catch the bus at South Street for downtown and the bus station.

The evening "cook" at the bus station had a drinking problem, and once a week or so would fail to show up for his evening shift. The manager started depending on my Grandma to stay and work a second shift as the cook!

When she got off the second shift, after a 16-hour day, the bus would no longer be running, and she would walk from downtown to their bungalow near Artesia. It was about eight miles.

When the U.S. entered the World War II, Grandma took a job at Douglas Aircraft working on the assembly line. When Gardena legalized poker, she started working in the card clubs where she continued to work until her 70s, selling chips and waiting tables for the "high rollers."

She would also carry $10,000.00 in cash and loan it out to "players" that ran out of money. There was a policy in place against loaning money to players, but Grandma thumbed her nose at the policy and "loan sharked" for about 25 years.

She remarried about 1948, and they purchased a new house in Lakewood. Grandma, using her tip money, had the loan paid off in three years. She used to tell me they could have purchased five acres near South and Downey for $5,000.00, and her husband said, "No," even though Grandma had saved the cash.

The day after Christmas in 1965, Grandma rented a cabin in Big Bear so we could go play in the snow. She took my brother and his friend, my cousin, my girlfriend and me. We stayed all week, which infuriated my step-grandpa.

Grandma told me years later, that a couple of weeks after we returned from Big Bear, she stopped by the bank to deposit several checks. The money in their account was gone!

That evening, when she returned home from work, Grandma

went into the bedroom, put on her housecoat and then walked into the living room where Grandpa was watching TV. She asked what happened to the money in their account, and Grandpa replied that he had taken it because he was mad that she had gone to Big Bear.

Grandma reached into her pocket, pulled out her .32-caliber handgun, and told him, "If half the money isn't back in the account tomorrow, I will kill you!"

I asked her once if she was serious, and she replied, "I would have shot him right between the eyes." They kept their money separate from that point forward.

Grandma was fun. She always had "ice cream" money for the grandkids and going to her house was always special.

After I got my driver's license, I loved going to her house for breakfast, pancakes and bacon.

My Grandma was probably the greatest influence in my life after my father died. She was a wonderful, strong and generous lady. Melissa and I always told her she would live to be 100 hundred years old. She died in April 2014 at 100 years, 4 months!

Chapter 52 -- My First Union Job

On August 3, 1970, I started my electrical apprenticeship. I was dispatched to Shell Oil Refinery in Wilmington. Upon signing my paperwork, I was issued a round piece of brass with a number stamped in it. This was to be used as your time card. When you came through the construction gate every morning, you would ask the guy at the gate for your number, and then at the end of the day you returned it. They would keep track of your comings and goings.

The first journeyman I was assigned to asked me if I was new? "My first job," I replied.

"You don't need tools; leave them in your vehicle."

Several days later I was assigned to a different journeyman, and the first thing he asked was, "Where are your tools?"

There were about a hundred electricians on this job, and several hundred other workers from the various trades. There was a superintendent that was a representative for the contractor, then a general foreman that oversaw seven foremen, and each foreman was in charge of 12-14 men on their crew.

The union also had a rep, a union steward, to see that everyone followed the union agreement. As I worked every day

I was trying to understand the hierarchy. The next journeyman I was assigned to didn't have a clue of what he was doing.

One day we were to bend three pieces of 4-inch aluminum conduit, and after spending a full eight hours on this project, he bent them all wrong, and we spent the next day bending three more pieces of conduit, and again he did it wrong. Eight years later I walked into Coast Cadillac and purchased a new Coupe de Ville, and he turned out to be our salesman!

The next journeyman I worked with was a big old farm boy from South Dakota. He grew up on the farm and now the farm was his, but he had local farmers take care of the wheat crops for him.

He told me he received around $32,000.00 a year from the farm and didn't really need to work. He wanted to move to Mexico and live on the beach. At lunchtime he would pull a Mexican newspaper from his lunch box and spend time reading it to improve his Spanish. Being fresh out of high school with five years of Spanish under my belt, I was able to help him in his reading.

There was a guy on our crew that was 65 and was going to retire after this job was finished. One day he climbed down a 85-foot tower where he was working. He sat down on the ground and died of an apparent heart attack!

My journeyman from South Dakota walked over to me, shook my hand and said this was not going to happen to him. He was quitting and moving to Mexico immediately! I never saw him again.

So again I was assigned to another journeyman. We were in the process of mounting an explosion-proof telephone cabinet on a steel column. We needed some clamps, and the two of us walked over to the parts trailer to retrieve some. As we started back to where we were working, the guys were scrambling and yelling for help.

As we approached the column that we were working on, a crowd had gathered. We made our way through and lying where we had been working was an insulator who had been working 35 feet above us. He had fallen, landing on his head and was dead. The right side of his head and face looked like "Jell-O." The job was shut down for the rest of the day. Had we not have gone for those clamps, he would of landed on us or right next to us.

Melissa and I were getting married in October. So one day I asked my foreman if I could leave at lunch the following day to get our blood tests. The following day I left at lunch with his permission. The following day I was back, worked all day without incident, and headed for the parking lot at the usual 3:10 p.m.

The following morning I asked for my "brass" as I entered the job site. "Your brass has been pulled," I was told.

"What does that mean?" I asked.

"You need to go and see the superintendent."

I walked over to the trailer, knocked on the door and gave him my name. "Here's your check," he said, "You're fired!" He turned and walked back in the trailer.

Baffled, I started to walk back toward the parking lot. My foreman and several others were approaching the construction trailers, and he asked, "Where are you going?"

"Home. I've been fired!

"For what?" they asked, and I told them I didn't know why.

Mike said, "Let's find out."

Mike walked up, knocked on the trailer door, and the "super" opened it up.

"Why are you firing my man?" he asks.

"Because he brassed out early yesterday."

Mike asked, "What time did you leave yesterday?"

"3:10, just like every day."

The new time to brass out was 3:20. I told everyone at lunch on Tuesday.

"Mike, I was not here at lunch on Tuesday. I went for my blood tests."

"That's right," he said, and he turned and told the "super" why I had left early.

The super said, "I don't care, he's fired!"

Well, now most of the foremen were there as well as the general foreman and union steward. Mike, my foreman, said to the super, "Then get my check, I quit!"

"Fine," said the super. "I'll get your check too."

The general foreman then said, "Get mine while you're at it, I quit, also!"

The super was now turning red. He was really pissed!

Well, the rest of the foremen that were now assembled all asked for their checks, "We all quit!"

The super walked back into the trailer and slammed the door! After several minutes, the door opened, and the "super" reappeared, red as a beet! He walked down the trailer steps, walked up to me and grabbed my check out of my hands! Seething he yelled at me, "Get to work!"

Boy, did I get an education at the age of 19.

Chapter 53 -- Montana 1971

Melissa's Dad, George, was born and raised in Helena, Montana. From our first date in 1969, George was always talking about Montana. His childhood adventures about growing up in Montana sounded like it was a terrific place, a place that I'd love to visit.

So in the summer of '71, Melissa and I were going to meet her parents in Helena. They only had a week, but Melissa and I had several weeks. Our plan was to take our time getting there, visiting Bryce Canyon, Zion National Park, Yellowstone, Jackson Hole and then on into Helena, Montana.

We were traveling in our VW Bus. Melissa had with her long straight hair, and I was sporting long hair and a beard. I hadn't had a barbershop haircut in more than a year.

We left Long Beach early one morning, and our plan was to drive to St. George, Utah, passing through Las Vegas without stopping. We had been in Vegas nine months earlier after the Barstow to Vegas motorcycle race.

During our first night in Vegas my new Yamaha motorcycle

was stolen out of the back of Melissa's parents' Datsun pick-up while we were at dinner! So I wanted no part of Vegas.

As we headed out Interstate 15, we left Nevada and were in the corner of Arizona, maybe ten miles or so from the Utah state line. As the sun was setting, and we were getting hungry, we spotted a small café at the edge of nowhere, Arizona.

We pulled in and entered to find a couple of local men sitting at the lunch counter. We grabbed a booth; there was no one else in the place. The waitress was nice, and the food was good.

Melissa pulled out our highway map, and we discussed various routes that we could take over the next couple of days. As we plotted our route, Melissa marked the map using a yellow felt pen. When she was finished marking up the map, she noticed that the marker had gone through the map and had marked up the table.

After trying some water and napkins, the marker would not come off the tabletop. We covered it up has the waitress brought us our check. I grabbed the check and walked up to the register as Melissa waited at the table. I paid the check and walked back to our booth.

As I sat down for a minute so Melissa could grab her stuff, the waitress walked back to our booth and placed our check back on the table as if we hadn't already paid. I noticed as she walked back behind the counter that the men setting there glanced at us over their shoulders.

I had no intention of paying for our meal twice, so Melissa and I got up, walked toward the register that was near the entrance, and as we approached we quickly darted out the door.

We Jumped into our VW bus and headed toward Utah as fast as we could. I was more worried about the tabletop than I was about them trying to get the extra couple of bucks from me. I don't think that bus ever went as fast as it did that next 10 miles.

As I had the pedal all the way to the floor, I kept looking in the mirror for someone following us when we finally passed into Utah.

Slowing back down to 65 m.p.h., we laughed about what had just happened. I guess they didn't like "hippies," but we left our mark on the table!

Pulling into St. George we looked for a place we might spend the night. We decided to sleep in our bus which was parked at the city park. It was very hot in St. George that night, and so we slept with the windows open. Awakening the next morning, we discovered that we had shared our bus with a bunch of mosquitoes. Again we couldn't wait to get on the road.

As we spent the next week traveling through our National Parks, we had a blast. Seeing this part of the country for the first time was magnificent. We shared food with others we met on the road, swam in the Yellowstone River with 15-20 other "hippies" who were out there too. We also visited some great museums and a few really cool Montana ghost towns.

When we reached Helena, Melissa's folks introduced us to friends and relatives that were part of the stories George had been telling me about for the last two years. We fly fished in the same creek that George had encountered a Grizzly Bear growing up.

One morning George took me over to meet an old friend of his. We walked up to the front door of this old Victorian house, and an older gentleman came to the door. George introduced me to Ian McDonald, a Hollywood actor who had appeared in many westerns during the forties and fifties. His best known part was that of "Frank Miller," the man who got off the train in the classic movie "High Noon," and who had come back to shoot down Marshall Will Kane.

This turned out to be a great trip, and Melissa and I came

back to the area several more times in the next few years.

Melissa Mosley Out on The Road In Our VW Bus 1971

Chapter 54 -- Soggy Dry Lake

In the early '70s, we enjoyed riding dirt bikes in the desert. We'd go camping in the winter, usually just for a weekend. We'd leave Friday after we all got off work and usually arrived just after dark. It was always so beautiful when we awoke early on Saturday mornings. It was so quiet, and the vastness of the empty desert was so awesome.

We'd ride and camp at Soggy, El Mirage, Palmdale and Red Rock Canyon. What was unique was that we had three couples whom we enjoyed, and they all had bikes. Since we seldom went with everyone, Melissa and I could ride one weekend with Judy and Ken, another weekend with Judy and Dean, but usually we went with Bob and Beth. All but Ken had graduated from Poly.

One weekend while heading across the Soggy lakebed, we came upon a bi-plane sitting at the edge of the dry lake in front of an old trailer. After stopping to check it out, a couple of older gentlemen came out, and we began to talk. Their plane was cool, and we had plenty of questions.

While we were talking, Melissa was sitting on the wheel of

the plane. As I looked down at her, I spotted a small sidewinder rattlesnake slithering quickly toward her foot. I grabbed her and yanked her out of the way just in the nick of time, and everyone thought I had gone mad grabbing her like that! But I pointed out the snake, and they understood. I saved her life.

The old guys asked if we wanted to go up in their plane. They would take us up for $5.00 per couple. We quickly agreed, and soon Melissa and I were flying over the desert while Bob and Beth waited their turn.

Bob and I would often take off on our bikes and get racing across the desert floor, wide open in fifth gear. This was a blast, and we'd cover a lot of desert quickly. We headed up a canyon on one of these rides, and we came across an old ghost town. We approached the town and stopped our bikes. Upon setting out on foot to do some exploring we were surprised by a man whose job it was to keep everyone out.

He told us that we weren't allowed to enter. The town had been built to shoot commercials and hopefully one day a movie. They were afraid of vandals and fire.

Another time the four of us headed out on a rather long ride. We decided to stop and take a break as we began to realize how far away from camp we had gone. And it was hot. As we made our way back, we knew the general direction back to camp, but we were a bit off line, and it was getting hotter and hotter.

Finally, off in the distance we spotted a windmill and headed toward it. As we approached the windmill we saw that it was on a 10x10 cement pad. It had a garden hose and was surrounded by a fence.

It was like an oasis to us as we climbed the fence. Turning on the hose bib, a cool stream of cold well water came shooting out from the well. The four of us stripped down to our underwear and sitting on the cement we relaxed and cooled ourselves off. It was great. We later dressed and headed back to camp for a couple of cold beers and a campfire dinner.

Chapter 55 -- Lost At Sea; My Surprise Party

It was a few days before my 21st birthday, and I'd finally be able to drink legally! Although, that hadn't stopped me or my friends since I was in 9th grade.

It was Saturday morning and my father-in-law George called to see if I wanted to go with him boating that day.

"Boating, what's going on?" I asked. Don, a guy that George worked with bought a 26-foot cabin cruiser and needed to move it to Redondo Beach. I asked Melissa, and she encouraged me to go. "It should be fun," she told me.

Well, a couple hours later I was picked up by George, Don, a guy named Vic and Melissa's brother Mike. "Should be gone two or three hours," I'm told.

We ended up driving down to Newport Beach, down to a marina, and we met the seller of the boat. Now as we approached the boat, my first thought was, "What a piece of crap!"

Well, they go over the boat from one end to the other, all the while the seller telling Don all the things that were wrong with this thing! I just wanted to get this over with, and it had already been several hours.

Finally Don says, "OK, we're done, let's cast off. Oh, and, by the way, only one of the motors runs, but it should get us there just fine. This boat has two six-cylinder in-board motors down in the hull."

Well, off we go, leaving Newport and on our way to Redondo Beach. "Shouldn't take but a couple of hours," I heard this three or four hours previously.

As we get out off the coast the wind was blowing a bit and there were some pretty good swells. This really made us move slower, and we were starting to get tossed about. An hour or so into the "cruise" the sun was starting to set. We hadn't made it to Long Beach yet, and there was something wrong with the engine. It was missing badly, and sputtering.

Mike, Melissa's brother, and I crawled down below and checked out the engine. We thought that perhaps the points were bad, and we checked for tools. A screwdriver, pliers and crescent wrench was all we found. With these tools it was enough to pull the points out of the motor that didn't run, and we installed them into the good engine. We got it to finally run, adjusting the points by sight, and we are off again.

By the time we were off of Long Beach a couple of us suggested that we dock here, and Don could take it the rest of the way the following day. It was now dark, still pretty choppy, and Don said that he wanted to press on "just a couple more hours."

We got past San Pedro, and were now about a mile off the coast of Palos Verdes. It was pitch black and the sea was tossing us all over the place. We estimated the swells were 15 feet high. We rode up the swell and then crashed down the other side.

Then we started to doubt whether this boat could withstand this pounding. Vic, who also worked with Don and my father-in-law George, was sitting below in the cabin and was scared to death! He told us he couldn't swim. The waves were pushing us in towards the rocks, as by that time we were trying to go away from the shoreline, and this attempt was making our forward progress very, very slow!

As we got closer to shore we could see the outline of a ship that had run aground years before. It looked really eerie!

Meanwhile, at our apartment on Grand, Melissa and most our friends were gathering for a surprise party, mine, for my 21st birthday! I was now several hours late!

Melissa's Dad was supposed to get me out of the house until 5:30 or 6:00! It was now 8:30 or 9:00 p.m., and no one knew where we were!

Melissa called the Coast Guard, and she was told that someone else had also called, and we were currently listed as "lost at sea!"

Back on the boat I was trying to figure out where I should swim to if we needed to abandon ship! As a big swell picked us up and cracked us down, the engine quit and all the lights went off.

I smelled smoke. Mike and I pulled the hatch cover open and the engine was now on fire!

Grabbing some rags and a towel we managed to smother the fire. The good engine now looked like it was gone!

Then it seemed like just a matter of time before we would be washed into the rocks off of PV! "Did the guy say what was wrong with the engine that didn't run?" Mike and I ask.

"No," was all Don said. "Is there a flashlight?" we ask. Someone found one in the cabin, and Mike and I started pulling off parts from the now burnt engine and putting them back on the "bad" engine. This was not easy with a screwdriver and pliers, especially as we were being tossed about. I guessed that we were around 100 yards off the rocks when Mike and I told Don to try and start the bad engine.

He cranked and cranked, and it finally started! The lights came back on also, and we were once again headed out to sea. After we felt that we were a safe distance off shore, we headed north and back toward Redondo Beach.

As we finally got around the Palos Verdes coast, the swells dropped off to about half the size as before. Finally, we saw the lights of the marina and made it the rest of the way, safely finding and pulling into the first place we could tie up.

As we departed, there was a little coffee shop nearby! We all headed to the phone booth and made our calls! It was 11:30!

When I called home, Melissa told me how worried everyone was, and that I missed my party! Did I want to ride back to Long Beach with her Dad and Brother?

"No, come get me," I said! "How about Bob? He's been waiting to hear that you guys are OK. That would be great!" said Melissa.

While I was waiting for Bob, I had my first cup of coffee! It just sounded good.

When Bob and I got back to the apartment, several had waited. I had a couple of glasses of wine and cranked up the stereo!

Chapter 56 -- Eldridge Street

A strange thing occurred sometime in 1973. Melissa and I moved into a duplex in Long Beach on Eldridge Street, just off of Long Beach Blvd. We had sold our house in North Long Beach due to terrible neighbors. I had met a great realtor named Don who had subsequently gotten us into a couple of foreclosures and an apartment building and was trying to find us a house in my old Bixby Knolls neighborhood. So we needed some place quick and decent to land.

Melissa's good friend Judy had just moved into one of her Dad's rentals across the street from her parents' house on Eldridge Street, where he had built two duplexes right next door to each other, a total of four units.

Judy and her new husband Ken let us know that the unit next door was available, and we decide to take it. My good friend Bob had just returned to the area from a year in Santa Cruz, and he was looking for a place to live. As it happened, the unit in front of ours was coming available, and Bob rented it. Then several months later Judy and Dean, another couple we used to double date with at Poly, moved into the last of the four units.

Bingo, four units rented and each had members from Poly class of '69. Only Judy's husband Ken was not a Poly grad. We weren't sure how this all happened, or how it would all play out, but somehow it worked really well.

We were all so busy that we seldom saw each other. Judy and Ken were just finishing college. Bob was going through an apprenticeship with the Carpenters Union, as was Dean, and I was nearing the end of my four-year apprenticeship with the Electrical Union.

I remember watching the "Searchers" with Ken on a Saturday afternoon and discussing buying dirt bikes. Mine had just been stolen, and I wanted another. Ken knew someone, and we ended up buying two new 360 Yamahas in a package deal.

Judy and Dean had just purchased two small houses on Redondo near Anaheim Street and were beginning to rehab them, and that took up most of their free time, although we did hit Joe Jost's together occasionally.

Bob was my best friend, so I saw him the most. Bob had a great stereo and a nice collection of albums, so it was very common for me to have a few beers and listen to music while I waited for Melissa to get home from work.

One Friday morning we woke up to rain. I drove to my job site, an apartment building in Belmont Shore, and they shut the job down due to it being too wet to work. I returned home, and thirty minutes later Bob had pulled into the driveway as well. His construction site was also shut down.

Bob and I went into his unit, turned on the stereo and began to have a beer when Dean walked up to the door and let us know that he was also rained out. Just as he joined us, another head popped around the corner, one of Bob's friends, a landscape helper, and he was also home for the day.

Well, after a bit of small talk and another morning beer, we decided that we should play poker. So with the rain pouring down outside we spent the next six or seven hours involved in some serious beer drinking and low stakes poker.

When Melissa and then Judy arrived home and came searching for us, we ordered pizza and finished off a great rainy day.

Bob and I were invited to a bachelor party one evening in Belmont Shore. Dave, a Poly grad of '68, was getting married, and I saw a bunch of guys from Poly that I hadn't seen since high school. I remember waking up at about 5:00 a.m. in the driveway of our duplex, glad that Bob drove that night.

Melissa and I got pregnant and then lost our baby at six months. Then we finally found the house we wanted in Bixby Knolls and moved on. Ken got his accounting degree, and they bought a house and moved out. Judy and Dean finished their rehab project and moved into one of the houses, and Bob bought a house on Eliot Lane in Belmont Heights and was gone.

Although the situation on Eldridge Street lasted less than a year, it was fun and memorable, just a stepping-stone for all of us.

Chapter 57 -- Twin Wheels

When I decided not to go to Long Beach State on a baseball scholarship in the fall of 1969, I had decided to become a Union Electrician. My Mom's second husband was in the Union and thought that construction might be my way forward. I liked the idea of working outside and moving from job to job.

As I applied to the Union for the apprenticeship, I took a job at Fiat until I could start working construction. The process was long, taking about 9 months. There were interviews, aptitude and dexterity tests. I was finally accepted and told to report for work on August 3rd, 1970.

We worked 40 hours a week and attended Long Beach City College two nights a week for 4 years. Every 6 months we received a 5% "upgrade" if we completed our work and school requirements. At the end of 4 years we took a Union/State test to become a Journeyman Electrician. I couldn't wait for that day to come.

I finished my school in June of '74 and then waited for the test date several weeks later.

The test was on a Saturday morning at 8:00 a.m. in downtown Los Angeles.

The morning of the test I drove our red '61 Porsche and arrived in the parking lot an hour early so I could relax and collect my thoughts before taking the 4-hour state exam.

I finished my exam early, turned it in and was told we would be notified by mail if we passed or failed.

The following week I anxiously checked the mail daily. Finally Thursday in the mail was an envelope with the return address from the IBEW L.U. 11.

I swallowed hard as I opened the letter! Four years of hard work I thought as I opened it up!

Congratulations it said, you passed with a score of 88%.

Wow, I was excited to be free after 4 years! I let Melissa know and we decided to celebrate Friday after work.

Friday Melissa and myself and my best friend Bob headed to Twin Wheels Steakhouse for Prime Rib and drinks.

The three of us were seated in a nice booth, ordered our drinks and looked over the menu.

It took a long time for her to return and take our order. She seemed confused and we realized that she had been drinking. We didn't mind at first, but as our order came out, she had several things to correct to make it right. Finally with the order correct we enjoyed our meal. Then we had cheesecake for dessert.

Anxious to leave, it took forever for her to bring our check. When she showed up and placed it on the table, it wasn't ours. Ten minutes later she walked by again, grabbing her and letting her know this was not our check, she picked it up and vanished again.

The next time we saw her, she placed change on the table and walked away. The couple across from us suggested that it was their change. They picked it up and headed for the door. She again came by and dropped off the right check, but vanished before we could pay!

We sat there for what seemed like forever, no sign of the waitress, I said to Melissa and Bob, "Let's get the hell out of here!" We got up and headed for the door, walking through the bar toward the door. As we approached the door, the Hostess was standing there and I figured "Busted."

The Hostess looked at me and said, "I was wondering how long before everyone got up and walked out!"

"Have a great evening," she said as we walked out the door, money still in my hand!

Chapter 58 -- Melissa's Pregnant

We were very excited to start a family! We waited about five years after our wedding so we could do our "hippie" thing. Finally, the big day had come for Melissa to get her pregnancy test. We were excited about the news and started making plans.

Everything seemed to be going great until the morning of March 20, 1975, six months into the pregnancy. As Melissa got up, she was spotting! We called the doctor and headed to Long Beach Community Hospital.

When the doctor showed up, Melissa was admitted and taken to a delivery room. I was instructed to wait outside the room for what seemed like hours.

Finally, I saw a nurse come out the door, and I could see she had a small bundle. It turned out that our baby had a problem with the umbilical cord. Our baby, Marshall Mosley, was gone!

We were told to wait several months before we could try again. We waited as instructed, and we then tried again. Once again Melissa went for a pregnancy test. I was at work, Sullivan Electric in North Long Beach, where I went every workday. I left my car and then drove a company truck to the job site.

When I arrived back at the shop, I walked toward our red '61 Porsche. As I approached, I saw a stuffed animal and a card sitting on the steering wheel of the Porsche. I knew at that point we were pregnant again.

As things progressed we started taking Lemaze classes once a week. On the way home from the hospital we would stop at Russell's and have burgers and dessert. Everything seemed good; however, I was a nervous wreck as the time approached. It seemed like all was going well, considering we had made it past the six-month period.

We had purchased a house in Bixby Knolls, my old neighborhood, on a corner lot with three bedrooms, two baths and a big den. We had the nursery painted and wallpapered. Melissa's folks had come down from San Francisco for the big day. As the weekend ended, Melissa's Dad had to leave, but her Mom stayed behind.

Early the next morning M'lis went into labor. We made the drive to Community Hospital, met the doctor and went into a delivery room. As the contractions came closer, the doctor seemed concerned. Again, I was sent out of the room, back to where I had sat a little more than a year earlier.

Well, I waited and waited; again it seemed like hours. Once again I waited, fearing the worst. When the doctor came from the room, he informed me that I had a new baby girl.

The umbilical cord was wrapped around the baby's neck, and with each contraction it was causing distress. So they took the baby with forceps!

When I finally got to see our baby, Mandi, she was a beautiful and healthy baby girl, but with a pointed head and bruises from the forceps. This really freaked me out! Our Bi-

Centennial baby... Mandi was a pleasure to raise and so enjoyable, but I never wanted to go through it again.

Seven years later, in the spring of 1983, to our surprise, Melissa was pregnant! We were excited -- however, I was very scared. But as the months slowly past, everything seemed to be going well. We had a different doctor, and this time Melissa was going to deliver at Long Beach Memorial Hospital.

We signed up for natural childbirth classes at Memorial, and then, once again, stopped at Russell's on our way home every week.

At the first class that we went to, I had an unexpected surprise. One of the teachers from Hughes was taking the classes also with his new, younger bride. Mr. Mays remembered me from Hughes, and this made the classes more enjoyable.

As our delivery day came closer, I really wanted this thing to be over. Our past experiences had really scared me, but when big the day came, we called the hospital and headed to Memorial.

I don't remember how long the labor was, but everything was going as planned. I was dressed in some kind of scrubs, with a mask on my face and helping Melissa "breathe."

They didn't hurry the doctor, because they thought this was Melissa's first delivery. But they soon realized that it wasn't, and they tried to slow her pushing as the doctor raced to the room.

When the doctor arrived, he assessed the situation and then told Melissa to push! One big push and Cari Beth came sliding out into my arms. Success! Everything finally went as planned. Not a day has gone by that I don't feel blessed with Mandi and Cari! But whew, I was done!

My Brother Chris

Chapter 59 -- "Lest We Forget"

My brother Chris was born December 28, 1953. We were pretty close growing up. We started out playing with Tonka Toys and with my American Flyer train set. We played cowboys using the arms of the couch for our horses, and many other make believe games we could come up with.

When I was about six, our parents bought us "cowboy outfits" that included leather chaps with a matching vest. Boy, we were in heaven!

Not long after this we moved to Elsinore where my Grandpa had a horse and cows. We thought we were becoming real cowboys. We also had a lot of small army men and tanks to play with, but our favorite was the cowboy and Indians, wagons and horses that came with the Fort Apache and western town set that we had. We would play with these for hours.

When we moved back to Long Beach in 1958, my Grandmother bought us complete Rams uniforms with helmets, shoulder pads, pants and jerseys. Our favorite time to play football all suited up was in the back yard on rainy days. It felt like we were real football players tackling each other in the rain. We had a blast!

In Long Beach we got for Christmas one year Mattel Fanner 50s cap guns and holsters and Mattel Winchester rifles. My Dad then built us a two-story playhouse in the back yard. We would have gunfights with one of us shooting from the "hayloft" while the other approached on foot.

Then the downstairs "sheriff's" office would hold the captive one in jail until he escaped out the side window. The pursuit and gunfight would start again.

As the mid-sixties came along, I started going to work with my Dad, and Chris stayed at home. When Dad suddenly passed away in 1966, we seemed to handle our grief in different and separate ways. I withdrew from the family and turned to my girlfriend and her family. My brother turned toward some of his friends, and they started leading him in a "medicated" way of numbing his pain.

We grew apart for some time. Several times we tried to reconnect as brothers, but things just weren't the same. In the early '70s as we both married and started families. We again became "brothers," bonding over our wives, daughters and horses. We became "cowboys" again.

We both purchased horses and starting riding and fishing together. We went to rodeos and "cutting" shows at Long Beach Arena. We would take our wives and little girls to Knott's Berry Farm, walk around the ghost town taking in the atmosphere of the old west.

We would then race home listening to the Eagles "Desperado" so we didn't miss the next installment of "Lonesome Dove" or "How the West Was Won." Life was good!

I remember Chris wanted to be a carpenter. I had a friend Steve who was a foreman on a framing crew, building houses in Torrance. I was helping him out framing because they could not get enough help and the pay was good.

I had him hire my brother, and everyone knew he was "green." The custom was to send the new guy looking for things that didn't exist: skyhook, toe nails, etc. I told Chris to look at me whenever they sent him for something, and I would give him a quick yes or no nod.

A couple of weeks after my brother came on board I overheard the owner of the company tell my friend Steve, "Boy, those Mosley Boys are really good!" I was really proud of Chris that day.

Unfortunately, the demons of my father caught up with Chris. While I was driving on the freeway in 1992, listening to KFI radio, they said there was a shooting in Long Beach. I said to myself, "Chris!" They finished the story, and said the victim's name was "Chris Mosley!"

My heart sank, but I knew it was him before they said his name. So much for notifying the family or next of kin. I never listened to KFI radio again. His life ended July 2, 1992.

It was also the last time I've cried.

My Brother Chris and I
Kernville, California
1980

Chapter 60 – Hidden Secret

Growing up in Long Beach, my childhood seemed great. I knew something wasn't quite normal.

My Dad had a drinking problem; I had figured that out on my own. I believe the problem was there for years, although I didn't acknowledge it at a young age.

I knew in junior high that there was something wrong. I would go to my Dad's shop on Saturdays, and he usually didn't stay with me for very long.

Bob the "chrome man" would stop by around 10:00 and off they would go around the corner to the 90/80 Club while I was left to my own devices.

His Saturdays with Bob became longer and longer.

At home, Dad often came home later and later every night. Mom tried to hide her concern from my brother and me. Dad was never mean, never abusive to any of us! I think that's why he could hide his drinking so well.

Another sign that I picked up on was the fact that Mom and Dad stopped coming to my baseball games. At first they would show up late, or in the middle of the game, but by the end of the season they no longer made it at all! The summer of 8th grade was the last time they saw me play any sport! Everything had fallen apart by then, Mom and Dad arguing, Dad coming home very late, us moving to my Grandma's house for a couple of weeks and then moving out of the house into an apartment nearby.

Mom finally got his Mom, Grandma Katie to intercede. Dad decided to seek help. He was placed into a hospital and taken off alcohol and restrained to a bed. He died two days later from heart failure due to the stress! Dad was 33 and I was in 9th grade at Hughes Junior High.

I dealt with his death, as well as Mom remarrying, as best I could. I spent most of my time at my girlfriend's house, her family becoming my surrogate family. I also worked after school so I wouldn't have to be home.

After graduating from Poly, Melissa and I dated and then married. Mom had divorced Ralph and wanted to move from the house and neighborhood. I was able to help in the process. Melissa and I had been buying and selling houses and our agent and friend Don was able to sell her house and find her a new place in Lakewood.

When the house was sold and we were helping mom move out of the house, I could remember Dad getting up in the morning and playing my Marty Robbins album on the Hi-Fi. El Paso, Big Iron and Cool Water were both our favorites.

A step away from the Hi-Fi was the linen closet where Mom kept clean towels and sheets. It was also the opening to the crawl space that led to under the house.

As Mom was removing the linens she found a bottle of Seagram's 7 stashed in the corner. Mom asked me to open up the lid to the crawl space and take a look below.

As I lifted the cover and stuck my head into the opening, I found what Mom thought I might find; dozens of empty Seagram's bottles.

I can't remember if I cleaned them out or if they could still be there!

I'm guessing that Dad always kept a bottle in the closet, maybe adding it to his coffee while listening to El Paso on the Hi-Fi. Dad's hidden secret!

Chapter 61 -- Jaws

The summer of '75 saw the release of the blockbuster movie "Jaws." Melissa's parents were visiting us from Redwood City, where her dad George worked at Marine World, Africa USA.

Melissa and I had purchased a house in my childhood neighborhood of Bixby Knolls, a great three-bedroom, two-bath home. It had a large den, and was on a corner, which we liked. It was 4438 Elm.

One Friday evening George got a call from someone at Marine World telling him that a fishing boat from Newport Beach had caught a large "Great White" shark, and it was going to be back in port first thing Saturday morning -- and could he drive down and get some pictures for Marine World.

At 5:30 the next morning I drove George to Newport Beach. As we arrived a small crowd had gathered to get a look at the shark. George gave security his business card, and we are quickly escorted onto the boat. Hanging there was a seven or eight foot "great white shark."

ABC news was there doing a news report with Inez Pedrosa. I was standing there watching her repeat the story several times for the camera and then interviewing various people on the boat.

About a week later my in-laws were back home in Redwood City, and Melissa told me her Dad was on the phone and wanted to speak with me. George had been sent down to Ventura to retrieve a mounted Great White shark that was on display in a bar. The bar was going to loan the shark to Marine World so they could create a shark display in the park and take advantage of the shark frenzy created by the movie "Jaws."

He wanted to know if I could drive to Ventura and help get the shark out of the bar and onto a truck so he could take it back to the park. So very early the next morning I drove to Ventura in my four-wheel drive Ford truck to meet George.

I hoped to be back home by 2:00 that afternoon. We needed to get it out of the bar before they opened at 10:00, I'm told as I arrived at our meeting place. I thought, how hard can it be to carry out a shark and put it in a truck?

As we reached the bar, the owner let us in and showed us the shark, sitting on a shelf behind the bar. Well, getting the shark off of the shelf and to the front door was easy enough.

Then the problem became apparent. There was a wall in front of the door so when someone came into the bar, one couldn't see the bar or its patrons. The shark would not turn the corner and make it outside. The wall had to come down and then be built back, all before 10:00 a.m.!

I saw then why I was there. So I grabbed some of my tools from the truck and took down the wooden wall that was stopping me from heading back to Long Beach. I got the wall down, and the shark was placed in the bed of my truck.

Using what nails I could salvage, I nailed the wall back into place just as the bar opened. All I needed to do then was drive George to the U-Haul dealer, and I'd be done.

We pulled into the rental yard and went into the office to rent the truck. We were almost set to go, and then the Marine World credit card they gave George was declined! After 30 minutes on the phone, it was decided that they would pay me to drive the shark to Redwood City.

Next, it was off to the hardware store where I purchased some rope to tie down the shark. We grabbed some lunch, and then it was off to Redwood City. We arrived sometime well after dark, maybe 9:30 or 10:00.

Several guys were there to check out the shark, and I think it was about midnight when we left the park. I drove George to his house and declined the invitation to stay the night. I was tired and just wanted to get back home.

I then drove the 400 miles or so back to Long Beach. I arrived more than 26 hours after I had left. I stopped at Hof's for some breakfast and then to the house to hit the "rack."

I don't remember receiving a check from Marine World, but just chalked it up to another adventure with my father-in-law, George.

George, Melissa and Myself
Convict Lake 1970

Chapter 62 -- Secret of Convict Lake

"The Secret of Convict Lake" was a movie from 1951 based on a prison break back in 1871. Twenty-nine prisoners escaped from Carson City, Nevada. Six made it to what is now "Convict Lake" just south of Mammoth and were killed.

I went to Convict in the summer of 1969 with Melissa and her family and a couple of our friends from Poly. Melissa's dad George took me fishing on the Lake and in doing so led me to believe that there was another secret of Convict Lake: How to catch a lot of bigger fish!

George had been fishing Convict since the early '50s. In those early days he met a man named "Bartholomew" who had been fishing at the lake since the 1930s. Over time George learned the secrets of fishing the lake, and over the next five or six years he passed those on to me, secrets that only I know today.

I spent about 25 years fishing Convict with friends, family, but mostly with George. We would get up just before daylight and head down to the boat dock; load our gear and head out "trolling" the deep waters of the lake.

Usually around 10:00 a.m. or so we'd come in for breakfast and then back to our boat. We would stay out there until dark if the wind stayed down, but usually the wind would come up in the afternoon and blow us off the lake!

The last time I fished with George was in the early '90s. We were staying in a cabin with George and his wife Nan, Melissa and I and our daughters Mandi and Cari. George was getting up there in age, around 78 or so, but he could still drive the boat around the lake.

As the wind came up this particular afternoon, later than usual, we decided to call it a day. As we pulled into the dock I grabbed the rope at the bow, guided the boat into the slip and tied us off. These boats were about 14 feet long, made out of wood and probably 50 years old with three bench seats.

George would sit on the rear seat and I'd fish from the front. At the end of the day we'd grab our tackle boxes, fishing poles, net and our worms. I climbed out of the boat with my gear and stood on the dock. George grabbed our stringer of fish, placed the worms in the net and grabbed his tackle box in one hand, fishing pole and net in the other.

Now, George always wore his felt cowboy hat while out fishing on the boat, being challenged for hair, and the high mountain sun could burn you quickly.

George started towards the front of the boat, stepping over the center seat. He almost made it but tripped on the seat and landed hard in the boat.

I asked him if he was OK, and he assured me that he was. His hat had flown off, and he dropped his tackle box and the fish. As he placed his hat on his head, he grabbed his fishing box and stood up, the pole and net still clutched in his right hand.

I could tell this hurt, but as he made his way out of the boat and onto the dock I looked at his pole. The pole that he clutched was now broken into three pieces and held together only by his fishing line. I couldn't help myself and burst into laughter. The look on his face, the tripping and landing face down in the boat and now his pole dangling in his hand was just too funny!

We walked to the truck and stowed the gear in the back, broken pole and all. I drove back to the cabin where we were greeted by the girls.

We walked in the door of the cabin, and I began relaying the events, George still grimacing in pain and me laughing as I told the tale. The thought of him standing there, holding pieces of the pole still makes me laugh. As George removed his hat, sitting on top of his head were the worms and their soil, minus the box, the worms wiggling all about. It was hilarious!

All of us started laughing. It was one of the funniest things I've ever seen! We all still laugh when the story is retold.

Me and Otis
Convict Lake

Chapter 63 -- Long Beach to Colorado, Part 1

Melissa and I married in 1970, a year and a half after we graduated from Poly. We lived in Belmont Shore, Belmont Heights, North Long Beach and finally Bixby Knolls.

During these five years we spent most of our free time riding motorcycles in the California desert, fishing and exploring the Eastern Sierra, running up and down Highway 49 in the Gold Country, up and down Highway 1, and traveling from southern Colorado up to the Canadian border in Montana. We loved it!

We were always sad returning home to Long Beach after having such great times on our many adventures. So we decided why not live in one of the places that made us happy!

We decided on southern Colorado. It had a great climate with four seasons, a tourist destination, a culture of Cowboys and Indians, and a true western heritage. Also, there were mountains, canyons, forests, rivers and lakes.

We listed our house at 4438 Elm with our friend Don after finding 25 acres in the Mancos Valley, half way between Cortez and Durango. Once our house sold, our plan was to head to Colorado and build a new house.

Don wanted to hold an open house on Sunday, so Melissa, our new baby Mandi and I headed off to the Crest Theater to see the latest John Wayne movie, "The Shootist." We enjoyed the movie, grabbed burgers at Russell's and then headed home.

Don met us at the door with the news that our house had sold! Now we were on our way!

Our friend Bob, a carpenter by trade, was going to take a month off and help me build the house. We arrived in Colorado on October 1, 1976, with my truck and camper, wife and baby, friend Bob and a lot of excitement. Another high school friend, Dean, lived in Cortez, and was also a carpenter. He told us with whom and how we should proceed with our build.

In the first week the site was graded. Bob and I had poured footings, and a block mason was laying the block foundation.

During the second and third weeks we were framing, installing trusses and laying shingles. Another friend from Long Beach, Mike, showed up for the third week and helped with the roofing and installation of windows. The month was up, and both Mike and Bob went back to Long Beach.

I wired the house while hiring a plumber to install water and drain lines. The weather turned cold, and Mandi, our baby, got sick. Since it was too cold to stay in our camper, I moved them into town at a local motel. After several days, Melissa decided to fly to San Francisco and stay with her parents while I finished the house.

Working night and day and soliciting occasional help from my friend Dean and his father-in-law Dick, we installed carpeting and linoleum during the week of Christmas. The house built in about 90 days!

I decided to meet Melissa in Long Beach at my Mom's for Christmas. We purchased a few light fixtures, and I picked up a few things that I had in storage, along with my Dad's tools on Christmas Eve. We woke up on Christmas morning, and after opening presents, I walked out to my truck. Everything was gone! Thieves had taken everything.

This reconfirmed to us that leaving Long Beach was indeed the right move for us. We drove to Colorado, a 14-hour drive, and when we arrived, it was snowing and everything was covered in snow. It was beautiful!

I carried Melissa and Mandi into our brand new house that evening. My brother and I had driven my friend Mike's U-Haul-type truck with our furniture to the property a couple of weeks earlier, and the next day we started moving in.

This part of Colorado was a bit of a culture shock! It was somewhere between 10 and 20 years behind southern California. You couldn't just walk in and buy a washer and dryer. One had to go to the Sears catalog store and order from them. It was the same with most other things as well.

During construction I had to fly to California to take care of a problem on a rental property that we had, and I asked Melissa to go to our Colorado bank and pick up a cash draw that we were due. Melissa went to pick it up, and the bank vice president told her she couldn't pick it up. There was some sort of a problem.

When I returned, my first visit was to the bank, hoping to straighten out the situation. When I walked into the VP's office, he shook my hand and handed me our check. It turned out that he thought that he should hand the check to me, not my wife!

Number one on my agenda, after completing the house, was purchasing a horse. I wanted to buy a registered Quarter Horse, preferably a "Buckskin." A guy I had met while building the house knew a horse trader south of town that could get any kind of horse I wanted.

Several days later I headed out to his place and rode a beautiful six-year-old registered mare. "A Buckskin!" After an hour of negotiating, I drove away the proud owner of my buckskin, 30 bales of hay, a rough-out saddle and a new bridle. I was ready to go! I later purchased Melissa a horse and with the new friends we had met, spent many days riding the high country in the Colorado mountains. I was in heaven.

To be continued...

My Grandpa Wilburn Mosley on his Harley

My Dad, Chuck Mosley 1949

About The Author

Chuck Mosley was born in 1951 in Long Beach, California. His Parents were both 17 years old and dropped out of Jordan High School their senior year in order to get married.

Chuck lived in north Long Beach until he was four years old. His parents purchased a new house in Palos Verdes where Chuck went to Kindergarten. He attended first grade in a one-room schoolhouse in Lake Elsinore before settling in Bixby Knolls where he would attend Los Cerritos Elementary, Hughes Jr. High and then Long Beach Poly where he graduated in 1969.

The author earned his degree at Long Beach City College and became a Union Electrician, Real Estate Investor, Contractor, Developer and Pilot.

Melissa Fryette married Chuck in 1970. They raised two daughters and moved to Colorado in 1996 where they still reside.

Chuck has always spent his spare time in the mountains riding horses, exploring ghost towns and fishing Convict Lake.

Made in the USA
Monee, IL
05 October 2023